A Wedding at The Cosy Cottage Café

A delightful romantic comedy to make you smile

Rachel Griffiths

Cosy Cottage Books

For my family, with love always. XXX

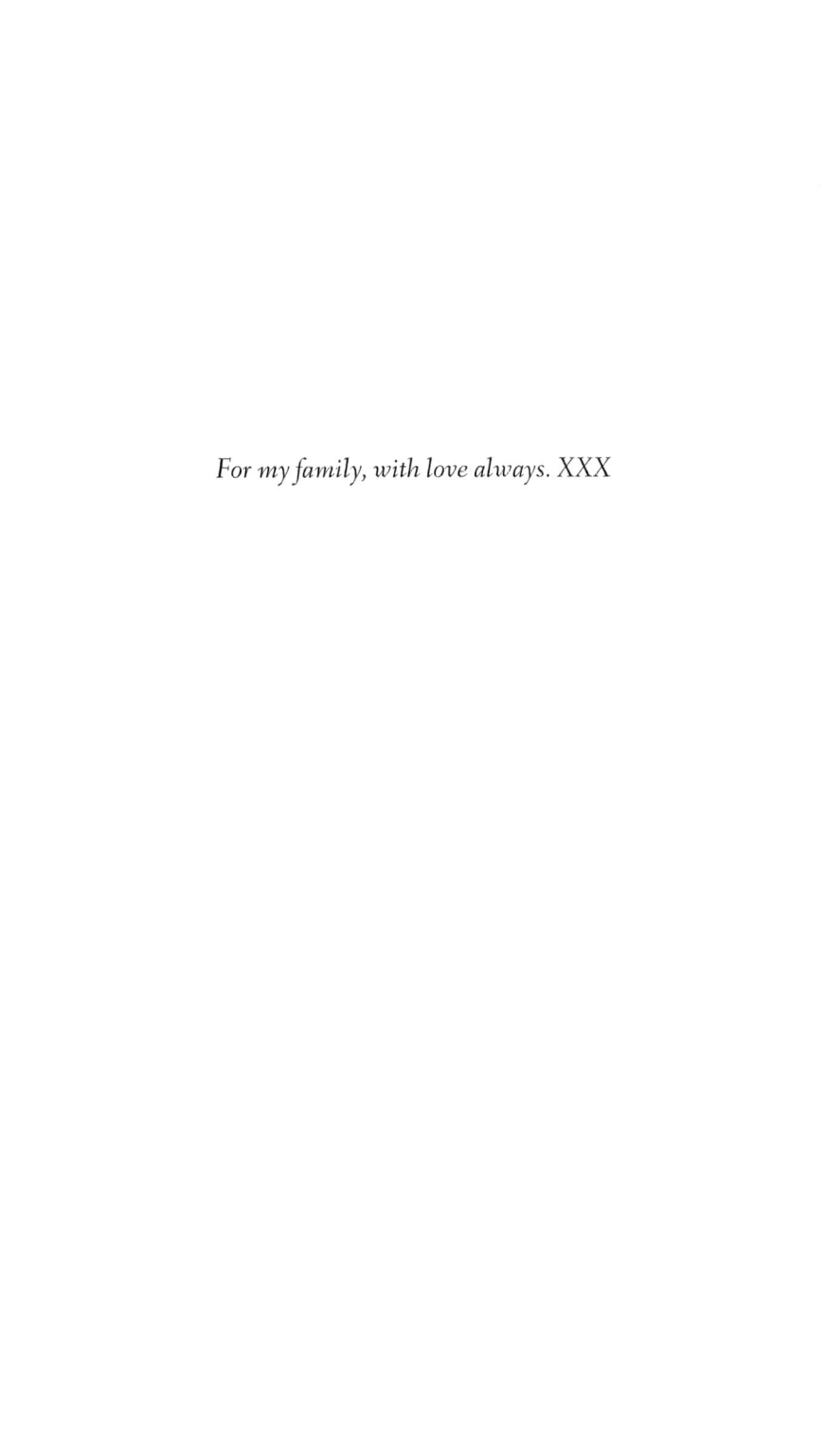

Cover Art by Stunning Book Covers

Copyright © by RachelA.Griffiths 2018

All rights reserved. This book or any portion thereof may not be reproduced or used in any manner whatsoever without the express written permission of the author, except for the use of brief quotations in a book review.

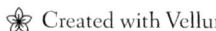 Created with Vellum

A Wedding at The Cosy Cottage Café

When Allie Jones' daughter, Mandy, arrives at The Cosy Cottage Café in tears one spring morning, Allie is concerned. She's been worried about her career-driven daughter for a while, and hopes she'll finally get to find out what's wrong.

Dawn Dix-Beaumont has her hands full with three young children, a husband who works from home and the guinea pig family that lives in her garden. She's happier than she's ever been, but is it too good to last?

Camilla Dix is madly in love with local vet Tom Stone, but she believes it's far too soon to be making long-term plans.

Honey Blackwell's boyfriend, Dane Ackerman, has secured his teaching post at Heatherlea Primary School and they've decided to live together. Everything seems to be working out well, until a member of Honey's household expresses a clear dislike for the handsome teacher.

And someone has been planning a proposal...
Join Allie and her friends this summer as cakes are baked, secrets are shared and surprises bring smiles and tears at The Cosy Cottage Café.

Contents

1.	Allie	1
2.	Dawn	5
3.	Camilla	10
4.	Honey	16
5.	Allie	19
6.	Dawn	24
7.	Camilla	27
8.	Allie	32
9.	Dawn	35
10.	Camilla	41
11.	Honey	44
12.	Allie	48
13.	Dawn	55
14.	Camilla	58
15.	Honey	63
16.	Allie	66
17.	Dawn	68
18.	Camilla	73
19.	Honey	76
20.	Allie	79
21.	Dawn	82
22.	Camilla	85
23.	Honey	88
24.	Allie	92
25.	Dawn	103
26.	Camilla	107

EPILOGUE - ONE SATURDAY IN JULY	119
Dear Reader,	131
Acknowledgments	133
About the Author	135
Also by Rachel Griffiths	137

Chapter 1

Allie

'OK, Mandy... sit there.' Allie Jones gestured at the battered old leather sofa in the corner of the café but her daughter didn't release her hand. 'Mandy?'

'Yes?'

'Sit there for a moment and I'll be right back.'

'Allie, tell me what you need and you can stay with Mandy.' Chris Monroe, Allie's boyfriend, placed a cool hand on her shoulder.

'Thank you. Can you get the brandy from the kitchen? It's in the top right cupboard above—'

'I know where it is.' He squeezed her shoulder. 'I'll be right back.'

She nodded as he padded away in his rabbit feet, still wearing the costume he'd put on for the Easter party at the café. From the waist up, he was normal Chris, but his legs dangled over the shoulders of a giant rabbit. Well, they were fake legs meant to resemble his, while his real legs looked like they belonged to the rabbit that was supposedly carrying him around. She was also conscious of the fact that she was still dressed as a fluffy yellow chick, something that had been great fun for the party, but now felt rather ridiculous.

Allie sat down next to her daughter. Mandy immediately buried her face in her hands, her shoulders shaking as she cried softly.

'What can I do, Mum?' Jordan, Allie's son, was still standing in the doorway, his face pale and his blue eyes wide.

'Sit down, love.'

Panic crossed his face.

'Or go help Max keep an eye on things outside.'

'Yes... good plan. But... uh... will Mandy be OK?'

Allie nodded, her heart aching, because even though Jordan was twenty-three — and now lived at the cottage attached to The Cosy Cottage Café with his boyfriend Maxwell Wilson — he was still her little boy.

'Yes, Mandy will be OK; she's home now. I'll have a chat with her, then come and find you.'

'Thanks Mum. See you later, Mandy.'

Jordan let himself out of the café then closed the door gently behind him, shutting out the sounds of the villagers of Heatherlea enjoying their Easter celebrations, just as Allie had been doing just ten minutes ago, before Mandy had arrived. Her twenty-four-year-old daughter — who had a successful career in publishing at a big London firm — turning up on her doorstep in a ball gown, her hair a bird's nest and her face streaked with tears, was something Allie had never wanted to see. In fact, it broke her heart.

'Mandy, are you going to tell me what's happened?' Allie rubbed her daughter's slender shoulders, exposed by the beautiful strapless damask dress.

Mandy let out a sound like one of Allie's cats might make. It was a pitiful squeak-come-sniffle.

'Here you are.' Chris was back and he handed Allie a glass of brandy. She looked at it, took a gulp, then patted Mandy's shoulder.

'I think you better drink this. It'll warm you up if nothing else. You're freezing, Mandy. Have you been out all night?' Panic rose in her throat at the thought that her beautiful daughter had indeed been out all night, alone and vulnerable.

Mandy didn't answer; instead she accepted the glass and sipped the spirit, wincing as she swallowed. But she kept drinking until she'd drained the glass.

'More?' Chris was hovering at Allie's side.

'Please.' She met his eyes and gratitude surged through her that he was there, that he'd returned to the village of Heatherlea last summer and that he loved her. Still. Even after all the years they'd been apart. Even after she'd married their mutual friend, Roger, and had two children by him.

Chris gently stroked her cheek then took the glass and went back through to the café kitchen. Allie turned back to Mandy and found her staring into space, her shoulders hunched, her eyes red and puffy. But at least the awful crying had stopped. For now.

'Mandy…'

'It's OK, Mum. Sorry to turn up like that but I didn't know what else to do.'

'How did you get here?'

'Early train.'

'Did you come straight from a party?'

Mandy nodded. 'It was an awards celebration for bestselling authors at a posh hotel with champagne, a sit-down meal and dancing.'

'Sounds lovely. But I take it that it wasn't lovely?' Allie watched Mandy closely. Since she'd last seen her daughter, her features were sharper, her arms more toned, as if she'd been working out and eating differently. Mandy had always been slim but she now had that gym-toned appearance that a lot of celebrities promoted.

'It was... at first. Then it all went wrong.' Mandy's lip trembled and a fat tear escaped from her right eye, ran down her cheek then plopped into her lap, staining her dress.

'How, love?' Allie took her hand.

'He's been lying to me all along, Mum. So many lies and I... I loved him so much.' Mandy's eyes brimmed with fresh tears. 'I really loved him!' She flung herself at Allie and sobbed in her arms, and Allie held her tight, wondering who she had to hunt down and punish for what he'd done to her baby girl.

Chapter 2

Dawn

'Do you think they're OK in there?' Dawn Dix-Beaumont asked her husband, Rick.

He glanced at the café then shook his head.

'You don't?' Dawn's voice rose with concern, so she coughed then made an effort to speak quieter as she asked, 'Really?'

'I didn't mean that they're not all right. What I meant was that Mandy did look quite upset but she's in the best place. So we shouldn't go interfering.'

'What? I had no intention of interfering.' She frowned at Rick but he smiled.

'I know that, angel. We have enough to deal with as it is.' He smiled down at their baby daughter who was fast asleep in her pram. 'We need to give them some space and I know how close you, Allie, Camilla and Honey are. You'll all want to rush to help Allie fix her daughter.'

Dawn nodded. 'You know me too well.'

He was right; her sister, Camilla Dix, and friend, Honey Blackwell, certainly would want to help in any way they could. They were close friends and always there for one another. But Rick was right; this was something Allie needed some space for and besides, Chris was with her.

'It might be a good time to head for home though.' He pointed at the café lawn where their young children Laura and James were racing around, their faces red, sweaty and chocolate covered.

'Oh goodness, yes. They both need a shower.' She smiled, her love for her children filling her chest. She felt so lucky to have such a wonderful husband and three beautiful children. Just the previous autumn, she'd been worried that it was all slipping away from her, as Rick had seemed distant and she'd suspected him of having an affair. He hadn't been, and had, in fact, been trying to protect her from his own worries, but now things were better than ever and they had a new baby too. Precious little Alison. She gazed at her baby's peaches and cream complexion and a familiar tingling spread through her as the let-down reflex kicked in.

'What is it?' Rick wrapped an arm around her shoulder. 'You've gone a bit flushed.'

'It's time for Alison to have a feed. Either that or I need to express.'

'No problem, my love. I'll round up the terrors and we can get going.'

He headed across the lawn in the direction of Laura and James, and Dawn watched as James shook his head and stamped his foot, then giggled as Rick hoisted him onto his shoulder and tickled him. Laura skipped towards her, looking exactly like a mini Spanish flamenco dancer in her Easter costume, except for the chocolate around her mouth, that was.

'Mummy!' James gasped as Rick tickled him again

when they arrived at her side. 'Daddy… says…' He squirmed. 'Daddy… stop!'

'Not until you say sorry for stamping.'

'I… wasn't… stamping!' James squeaked between breaths.

'I saw you stamp, James.' Dawn said, then she reached under his arm pit and wriggled her fingers.

'No, Mummy, no! Not you too!'

When Dawn and Rick stopped tickling James, and Rick set him down on his feet on the grass, James caught his breath.

'I wasn't stamping, Mummy, I promise. I was showing Daddy how Laura's supposed to do her mingo dancing.'

'I'm not a mingo dancer, James, it's flamenco!' Laura scowled at her younger brother, suddenly eighteen not eight, and Rick met Dawn's eyes.

'Looks like it could be a long afternoon.'

'Indeed. For you at least.'

'What's that supposed to mean?' Rick kissed her cheek.

'Well I need to feed the baby then take a nap. All the fresh air has worn me out.'

Rick sighed then kissed her again. 'You don't think your mother will want them for a few hours do you?'

'I have no idea… however…' Dawn waved her sister, Camilla over. 'Hey best big sister ever, I have a favour to ask.'

Camilla smiled. 'Anything.'

'You think you could watch Laura and James for a bit.'

'Pleeeassse, Aunty Camilla!' Laura took her aunt's hand. 'We'll be so good.'

'Can I play with Hairy Pawter?' James asked, pointing at the large British bulldog currently snoring at his owner, Tom Stone's, feet.

Camilla looked at her boyfriend, Tom, who was also the village vet, then back at her niece and nephew. 'I don't see why not. We didn't have anything else planned.'

'Yay!' James ran over to Tom and Laura soon followed.

'Are you sure?' Dawn asked her sister.

'Of course. You two look like you need a sleep. I'll take them back, make them wash that chocolate off then give them some tea before bringing them back.'

'Thank you so much.'

'What are big sisters for?' Camilla wiggled her perfectly shaped black eyebrows. 'You think they're all right in there?' She nodded at the café.

'I hope so,' Dawn replied.

'Like I told my wife, Camilla, you need to give them some space.'

Camilla's eyebrows rose slightly as she evaluated what Rick had just said.

Rick held up a hand. 'I also told her that I didn't mean to sound patronizing. I just meant that Allie has Chris and they probably need some time alone with Mandy. If we all go rushing in there, it'll likely be too much for Mandy and right now, she needs her mum.'

'You're right, Rick. It's hard to take a step back though.' Camilla shrugged. 'I'll text Allie later and see if we can help at all.'

'I'll just grab the box of books the children won.'

Rick went over to the band, who were set up in the corner of the café lawn, and picked up the box of books that James had won in the Easter egg hunt.

'Are we ready to go?' he asked when he returned to Dawn's side.

'Yes, let's get some sleep.' Dawn hugged Camilla. 'Thanks, sis, and any problems, let me know straight away.'

'We'll be fine. Besides, Tom's a vet so he knows first aid.'

'What?' Dawn blurted before she could stop herself.

Camilla giggled. 'Just teasing. Your children will be safe with us and I promise no first aid will be required. Now go and get some rest!'

Dawn pushed the pram down the path and through the café gate, then out onto the street. She glanced back at her children, who were stroking Hairy Pawter as he lifted his front paws in turn, then at the café.

'They'll be fine.' Rick hoisted the box of books onto his hip, then slid his free hand around her waist. 'All of them.'

'I hope so, Rick. I really do.'

Then they made their way home to catch up on some much-needed rest.

Chapter 3

Camilla

'Aunty Camilla?'

'Yes, James?'

Camilla smiled down at her nephew as he tugged at her hand.

'Is Hairy Pawter our cousin now?'

Camilla glanced at Tom and he shrugged, clearly as puzzled as she was by James's question. 'Because Laura said that Tom's our new uncle.'

Camilla stopped walking and took a deep breath.

'Tom is my...'

What? Boyfriend? Partner? Lover? BAE?

'We are a couple now, James.' Tom jumped in and saved Camilla from her quandary. 'So seeing as how HP is my... BFF, then I guess he's now your cousin. If that's how you want to think about him.' Tom flashed a grin at Camilla and she smiled in return.

'Yay!' James hopped on the spot causing the brown towel pinned to his shoulders as a cape, to float behind him. 'We have a cousin, Laura. James Skytalker has a cousin!'

A Wedding at The Cosy Cottage Café

'Don't be silly, James, HP can't be our cousin. He's just a dog. And you're James Dix-Beaumont not Skytalker. That's just your costume.'

HP gazed up at them, his fat pink tongue dangling out the side of his mouth, then he lifted a paw and offered it to Laura.

'I think he's trying to tell you something,' Tom said.

Laura crouched down next to HP. 'What is it boy?'

'He doesn't like being called *just a dog*, Laura, you silly billy.' James blew a raspberry. 'He wants to be our cousin.'

Laura kissed HP's paw then released him and stood up. She looked at Camilla and at Tom then rolled her eyes in James's direction.

'OK, James, HP is our cousin. Whatever.'

As Laura and James ran on ahead, Camilla tucked her arm into Tom's.

'Well that was interesting.'

'Which bit? The part where you didn't know what to call me, or the part where HP became an official family member?'

'Uh… all of it really. I mean… I think of HP as my family now and I couldn't imagine if he wasn't around, just as I couldn't imagine not seeing you every…' She bit her lip.

'Go on… finish what you were going to say.' Tom raised her hand and kissed it.

'Sorry, I'm still getting used to this. What I was going to say is that I couldn't bear not seeing you every day, Tom. Well, except for when you go back to Brighton and see your family and when you go on vet courses and… gosh, I know there will be times when I don't see you every day, but I know I will see you again, so it's OK… But if I wasn't going to see you again, I don't know what I'd do.'

Tom stopped walking and turned to her.

'Camilla, it's OK.' He smiled then glanced left to check on the children, who were currently studying a beetle that was making its way along the dry-stone wall outside the village church. He gave Camilla a quick kiss that sent warmth flooding through her. 'I need to see you every day too. You, beautiful lady, have become my whole world.'

'You're my world, Tom. I'm so glad you came to live in Heatherlea.' She gazed into his soft brown eyes, knowing she would never tire of looking at him.

'Me too.' He kissed her again. 'But I do think we need to decide upon an appropriate term.'

'A term?'

'You need to know what to call me if people ask.'

'What do you call me?'

'Camilla.'

She gave his arm a mock punch. 'No, how do you describe me to people?'

'I'll be honest; I've skirted labels by saying that I'm dating you, or in a relationship with you, or that we're a couple. Calling you my girlfriend feels a bit… young, I guess, and calling you my partner feels quite formal.'

Camilla nodded.

'Perhaps…' Tom's brown eyes seemed to sparkle with mischief as he held her gaze.

'Perhaps what?'

'Perhaps we need to have a new way to refer to each other.'

'A new way?'

He inclined his head. 'Yes. You know… a more permanent way.'

Camilla frowned as she tried to work out what he

meant. What other names were there for the person you were in a relationship with?

Tom squeezed her hand. 'Camilla what I'm trying to say is—'

'Aunty Camilla!' Laura's scream cut him off.

Camilla tugged her hand from Tom's and ran towards her niece.

'Oh my god, Laura, what's wrong?'

She looked at her eight-year-old niece, who she swore resembled Dawn more every day, and winced at the tears brimming in her pretty eyes.

'A wasp stung me.'

'What? Where?' Camilla stroked her niece's soft hair as Laura lifted the hem of her flamenco costume and showed Camilla her ankle. 'Oh, sweetheart.'

Camilla knelt next to Laura and gave her a hug just as Tom and HP arrived at their side.

'I have some cream at the surgery that will take the pain away, and I'm pretty certain Auntie Camilla has some ice cream at her cottage that will make you feel better.'

'James, what's wrong?' Camilla realized that her nephew was standing behind Laura and that he had tears running down his cheeks too.

He sniffed, his small shoulders shaking.

'I should have protected Laura.'

'How, sweetheart?'

'With my powers.' He gestured at his costume. 'But I didn't see the wasp and now she's sad and hurt and... I'm a bad brother.'

Camilla reached out and pulled him into their hug. 'James, you are not a bad brother. Wasps sting people all the time and no amount of super powers will change that. Isn't that right, Tom?'

'Indeed it is.' Tom was holding HP on a tight lead because he was trying to get to the children, no doubt to shower them with slobbery doggy kisses to make them feel better.

'HP is worried about you both.'

James turned and rubbed the bulldog's silky ears. 'We're OK, HP. Don't worry.'

Camilla got up, and with a child holding each hand, they made their way to Tom's veterinary surgery. She'd only had her sister's children for twenty minutes and already they were both in tears. She might be their loving auntie but she needed to make sure that they both had smiles on their faces when they returned to their parents later. Dawn and Rick were worn out and she wanted to help them as much as she could, but they'd never let her look after Laura and James if they returned home with horror stories of being stung and crying in the street.

Dawn had told her numerous times that parenting was wonderful but really hard work. Camilla hadn't always believed it, wondering how such tiny human beings could cause a problem for anyone, but the more time she spent with Laura and James, the more she admired her younger sister.

Thank goodness that she and Tom hadn't had a serious discussion about having children of their own. They'd cooed over baby Alison, and hinted that it could be something they'd consider in the future — likely testing the water with each other — but no concrete plans had been made. Which was just as well, because Camilla was inclined to believe that she'd be a disaster at the whole thing.

Better to be a favourite auntie and leave it at that.

When they arrived at the surgery and Tom unlocked

the door then ushered them all inside, Camilla realized that he hadn't had a chance to finish what he was about to say. That conversation would have to wait, because Laura had a wasp sting that needed treating and James needed ice cream to put the smile back on his sweet little face.

Chapter 4

Honey

Honey stretched out her arms and legs, enjoying the delicious sensations that coursed through her limbs. Nothing like a Bank Holiday Monday to make a woman feel relaxed. The bedroom was golden with the early morning sunlight that was filtering through the curtains and whispering of a beautiful day ahead.

The duvet next to her moved and dark hair appeared first, followed by Dane's handsome face and bright blue eyes framed with thick black lashes.

'Good morning, roomie.' He grinned lazily at her, his left cheek featuring a pillow crease and his stubble already casting a dark shadow over his strong jaw.

Honey leant towards him and kissed the bridge of his nose, widened by a break in a rugby game, then she kissed his full lips, the top one with its thin white scar where someone in the opposing team had caught him with their knee. She loved his scars, his small imperfections that made him who he was. To her, he was perfect in every way.

He pulled her into his arms and kissed her back, and she breathed him in, the warm male scent laced with yesterday's citrus-ginger cologne, a combination that made her stomach flip.

'Mmmm. Good morning, to you too, roomie.'

They lay back on the pillows, holding hands, enjoying the birdsong from outside that seeped through the open window. Honey always left the bedroom window open a crack, even in winter, because she liked to have fresh air in her room.

'What shall we do today?' Dane asked as he played with the fingers of her left hand, straightening each one out in turn then planting kisses on the tips.

'I don't mind.' She turned to peer at his profile and her heart fluttered. She couldn't believe her luck. This beautiful man with his sapphire eyes, his short thick dark hair and his strong broad shoulders was hers. Her lover. Her friend. Her partner in crime. Dane had agreed to move in with her, now that he was staying in the village — after securing his teaching post at the local primary school — and she was beyond delighted.

'I can tell you one thing, Honey.'

'You can?'

He nodded. 'I'm not doing any school work today.'

'You're not?'

'Nope. Today is reserved.'

'Ooh! Reserved for what?'

'You and me.'

'Dane, that's so good to hear.'

She rolled onto her side and snuggled up to him, winding her arm over his chest, her leg over his. Dane had worked so hard to secure a permanent position at the local primary school that Honey had been worried about him. In fact, he had recently admitted to being aware that he'd neglected everything else. But now he'd established himself,

Honey hoped he'd be able to find more of a work-life balance.

'And in that case... how about if we start moving your things in here?' She ran her fingers over his chest, stroking the dusting of black hair on his chest then slowly following the line that ran down to his navel and beyond.

'Hey!' He lifted her chin with his forefinger.

'What?'

'I asked you a question. Didn't you hear me?'

'No... I, uh, was thinking about something.'

'Were you now?'

He laughed then rolled her onto her back and leant over her, his blue eyes scanning her face.

'I think I know what you were thinking about but I'll have to test the theory.'

Honey smiled as he gently ran a finger over her cheeks then over her lips and down over her chin to the hollow of her throat, where he pressed a soft kiss.

'I asked you, Honey, if we should have a good breakfast first, as moving requires a lot of energy.'

'Definitely. I have lots of eggs, so I'm sure I can whip something up.'

'No you don't. I'll make breakfast.'

'Are you sure?'

He nodded. 'Absolutely.'

'Before you go...' She smiled at him.

'Before I go?'

'One more kiss?'

'Just one more.'

She rolled onto her side again then he kissed her, and all thoughts of making breakfast temporarily slipped from their minds.

Chapter 5

Allie

Allie walked into the kitchen of the cottage she shared with Chris and shivered. It wasn't cold in there, but she felt cold because she'd barely slept a wink. All night long, thoughts about Mandy and how upset she was had raced through Allie's mind and she'd wondered if this could have been avoided in some way.

'Morning.' Chris looked up from his iPad. He was sitting at the kitchen table near the window.

'Is that coffee fresh?'

'It is indeed.'

She sat down as he poured the dark brown steaming beverage into a large mug then handed it to her.

'Thank you. What time did you get up?'

'About half an hour ago.'

She glanced at the clock.

'You were up at six?'

'Yeah, I didn't sleep that well to be honest.'

'I'm surprised I didn't hear you get up.'

'I was as quiet as I could be because I didn't want to disturb you after the awful night you had.'

'I know... I tossed and turned. I'm just so worried about Mandy.'

Chris reached out and squeezed her hand. His touch was warm and reassuring and she sent out a silent thank you that he'd come back to her. He made her feel safe but also that she could achieve anything. He saw her in the way she'd always wanted to see herself and she loved him for it.

'Mandy will be OK. You know that don't you? She has you and Jordan, and now, she also has me.'

'Thank you.'

'Hey, don't thank me. I'm your partner, remember, and I love you more than anything, Allie. You're my everything.'

'Do you love me more than writing?' She used their favourite joke, trying to lighten the heaviness that had weighed her down since Mandy had turned up at the café yesterday.

Chris frowned, pouted, then met her eyes.

'You know... I think I do. But only just.'

They smiled at each other and she took comfort from his familiar handsome features, her very own George Clooney lookalike. But without the baby twins that Mr Clooney had, thankfully. In her early forties and with two grown up children, Allie did not fancy adding to her brood, and seeing as how Chris had agreed that he was happy to continue as they were, there would be no tiny feet pattering around in the cottage. It had formerly belonged to Chris's mother, and even now, Allie sometimes thought of it as *Mrs Monroe's cottage*. Not that it mattered, because Allie was happily settled there with Chris. Knowing that she would fall asleep in his arms every night and wake to find him next to her was the best feeling in the world.

'Allie, I've been thinking.'

She sipped her drink, savouring the delicious aroma of the good quality coffee Chris insisted they buy.

'I...' He ran a hand through his salt and pepper hair. 'I think that we should... now that we're together and have been for a while, I was thinking it might be a good idea if we...'

Allie peered at him over her mug.

His cheeks were flushed and he was worrying his bottom lip.

'What is it? You look worried. Chris, is everything OK?'

He nodded. 'It is. Absolutely. I'm just trying to find the right way to say this. But perhaps here and now isn't the right time. It should be more... special. Yes.' He nodded as if listening to an internal voice.

A creak from above their heads made them both look up.

'More special? What should be *more special*?'

Another creak from above.

Allie put her mug down on the table and stood up. Chris held up a hand. 'She might just be using the bathroom. Don't go up just yet in case she goes back to bed.'

'But what if she needs me?'

'Then she'll come down. She probably needs to catch up on some sleep too.'

Allie sat down again. 'You're right. I'm like one of those space shuttle mums.'

'A what?'

'You know... the ones who hover around their children nervously all the time, waiting to hug them at the first sign of a frown or a wobbly lip.'

Chris's lips twitched.

'What's amusing you?'

'I think you mean helicopter.'

'Helicopter what?'

'Helicopter mums. They're the ones who hover round their children.'

Allie waved a hand. 'Yes, that's what I meant. Then again, if I was more attentive and if I had gone to London more often then I'd probably have spotted that something wasn't right in my daughter's life. I could have saved her from this.'

'No, you couldn't. Mandy is an adult now, Allie, and she has her own life in London. She wouldn't have appreciated you popping in every five minutes and even if you had, you couldn't have controlled her social circle or who she dated.'

Allie drained her coffee then wrapped both hands around the empty mug.

'I know. You're right. I just feel so guilty. Even though she is a grown woman, she'll still always be my baby and all I want is to see her happy. Jordan is happy here in Heatherlea with Max and they're such a perfect match. But Mandy has always been such a go-getter, so determined and driven. I never thought she'd be the one to end up destroyed by love.'

'Did she tell you any more about what happened?'

Allie shook her head. After they'd brought Mandy back from the café, Chris had made himself scarce by going out to see a friend, while Allie had tried to talk to her daughter. But Mandy had been too upset to explain properly and in the end, Allie had thought a long hot bubble bath and a very early night would be of more benefit to Mandy than trying to talk it all through. Sometimes it was better to sleep on something and return to it with a fresh mind and heart. Allie had ended up falling asleep on the sofa, only waking when Chris had come home and led her up to bed.

'She needed to wash the day away and to rest. Perhaps she'll tell me today. Perhaps she won't. But either way, I'm hoping she'll agree to stay for a while to get herself together.'

'I'm sure she will.'

Allie got up and went around the table to Chris then wrapped her arms around his shoulders and buried her face in his hair. He slid his strong arms around her waist and held her tight. They stayed that way for a while, as the boards above their head creaked, signalling Mandy's return to bed, and outside a lawnmower started up as someone made the most of the bank holiday sunshine.

'I don't know what I'd do without you, Chris.' Allie spoke into his hair, breathing in his sandalwood shampoo and his own very special scent.

'You, my love, will never have to find out.'

Chris turned her around so she sat on his lap then kissed her softly. And although he'd never be able to stop her worrying completely, with him at her side, Allie knew she would be able to deal with whatever came her way.

Chapter 6

Dawn

Dawn pushed the pram along the pavement, taking deep breaths of the cool fresh air. It was a beautiful April morning and she was glad to be outside. She'd left Rick and the children in bed, believing that after an exciting party at the café then an afternoon spent with Camilla and Tom, Laura and James could do with a lie-in. Rick had been up with her in the night when she'd seen to Alison, so she thought he deserved some more sleep, and Dawn had had to get up anyway to feed and change the baby at six.

When she'd opened the curtains downstairs to find such a glorious morning, she'd decided to pop Alison in the pram and make the most of it. She had an ulterior motive, of course, hoping it would make Alison sleep through the morning so she could spend some time with Laura and James, but a walk would also help get her fitness up and get her back in shape after her pregnancy. She'd need to be fit and healthy to run around after three children, after all.

She walked briskly, imagining the toning effect upon

her legs and belly, and almost ran straight over a squashed black shape on the pavement at the end of her street.

'What the hell is that?' She peered around the pram, wondering if someone had lost a jumper or a scarf on their way home from the Easter party at The Cosy Cottage Café. But no... It was something else, something far more distressing than an item of clothing.

'Oh, Alison, what are we going to do?' She looked beneath the hood of the pram at her tiny daughter and Alison blinked her grey eyes, as if she was giving the matter some serious consideration. 'I can't really do much about it can I, as I have you with me and I don't want to go back yet, because if I do, then I'll wake everyone up. We'll have to come up with an alternative plan.'

She put the brake on the pram, then looked around. She spotted a long stick in the grass that edged the pavement. After she'd picked it up, she gingerly poked at the black shape. It moved with a squelch and she grimaced. Not good, not good at all. No sign of life there. The poor thing must have crawled from the road, or been struck with such a force that it had ended up on the pavement. With a flick of her wrist, she moved the shape across to the grass. At least it was out of the way and if anyone came along, they wouldn't step on it. Hopefully, no one else would even see it.

That would have to do for now.

'Come on then, Alison. Let's go see Auntie Honey and ask what she thinks we should do.'

Honey's house was the closest and she hoped that her friend would probably be up doing yoga or feeding her chickens, so she'd head there first.

She clicked off the pram brake then walked in the direction of Honey's cottage. The day hadn't exactly got off to the positive start she'd expected, but that was life, and if she could spare someone from the upset of seeing what she just had, then that was what she would do.

Chapter 7

Camilla

'How about we do something special today?' Tom asked as he poured boiling water into the teapot and swirled it around.

'Like what?' Camilla carried the plate of toast to the table then sat down. The French doors were open and outside, HP was sniffing around the decking. Mild spring air drifted into the kitchen, carrying the heavenly scents of sweetpeas and the sharp floral aroma of lavender from Tom's pots. Camilla stifled a yawn, not wanting to put a dampener on Tom's plans. The previous day, with the Easter party at the café, as well as taking care of Laura and James until the evening, had been tiring and she'd imagined a relaxing day with Tom and HP at his cottage, possibly with a pub lunch at The Red Fox then an afternoon nap.

Tom brought the teapot and mugs to the table and sat opposite her.

'We could go somewhere. Perhaps for a walk at a park or—'

'Aren't you supposed to be on call?'

Camilla spread some of Allie's homemade strawberry

jam onto a piece of toast. The sweet fruity conserve was like summer in a jar, and this morning, the smell of the strawberries seemed to be stronger than usual.

'I am but I wasn't thinking of going too far. It's just nice to get out and about sometimes. And it is a bank holiday.'

'And you feel that you should be doing something?'

He smiled and his soft brown eyes crinkled at the corners.

'We don't have to.'

'I like the idea, but let's have breakfast and shower first then decide what to do.'

Tom glanced at the clock on the kitchen wall. 'It is still early, I guess.'

Breakfast eaten, washed down with three mugs of tea, dishwasher loaded and switched on, Camilla headed upstairs for a shower. She loved being at Tom's cottage, with the personal touches like the paintings by local artists — including Honey — and neutral rugs and furnishings, with the scents of his washing powder and shower gel that hung about his towels and bathroom, and with the whisper of his aftershave in the bedroom. It all combined to make her realize how much she cared about him and how far they'd come as a couple. She'd been so keen to stay single before she'd met Tom, convinced that she'd never meet a man who would change that. Years of her mother ranting about her father — who'd walked out when Camilla and Dawn were children, leaving their mother to struggle alone — had made Camilla harden her heart to love. Then Tom had come to the village with HP and bit-by-bit, they'd both stolen her heart.

Life was so different to how she'd once thought it would be and her father's return to Heatherlea in the autumn, followed by his reunion with her mother, had been a big part of that. Laurence Beaumont was now happily living with his ex wife and had morphed from the fun-loving party guy Camilla had been brought up to believe he was, into a loving partner and doting grandfather. The best thing about it all for Camilla was seeing her mum and Dawn so happy at his return. It was as if he'd never been away and yet... the past could never be undone or forgotten. She shrugged. Perhaps it was meant to be that way so that when he came back to Heatherlea, his relationship with his family would be all the better for it.

Camilla had maintained her independence by keeping her cottage while Tom had his, but they spent most nights together. She still experienced moments of fear, when she'd worry that Tom might change his mind about her and that he'd walk away, but they were becoming less frequent the more time they spent together. Tom had won her trust and confidence in a way no man ever had done before and she hoped with all her heart that nothing would spoil their relationship.

When they'd first become close, she'd found out that Tom was still married —although he'd been separated from his wife for some time — and it thrown her into a sea of doubt about their relationship. But the divorce had been finalized just after Christmas, his ex was heavily pregnant by her new partner at the time, and Tom had reassured Camilla that his marriage had been over long ago in every way except on paper.

She walked into the bathroom and caught sight of her reflection in the mirrored cabinet above the sink. Her face was so pale, and were those dark shadows under her eyes? Perhaps yesterday had worn her out more than she'd realized. Nothing a long hot shower and a coat of concealer wouldn't sort out.

She opened the cubicle door and turned on the shower then undressed while the water heated up. Camilla never liked to get straight under the spray, as being chilled wasn't something she enjoyed. Tom said a quick blast under the cold water was invigorating but she couldn't agree with that at all. Once the cubicle was nice and steamy, she opened the door, stepped in and let the hot water wash her thoughts away.

∼

'Camilla?'

Tom was standing outside the shower cubicle when Camilla opened the door. He opened up a large fluffy towel and she stepped into it, smiling as he wrapped it around her then hugged her tight.

'Mmmm. That's lovely, thank you.'

'Can't have you getting cold, can we?'

He lifted the corner of the towel and gently wiped her face.

'I was thinking that we could just take it easy this morning if you like, then perhaps head out later. What do you think? You look a bit peaky and I hope you're not coming down with something.'

'So do I. If I am, it's likely something Laura and James passed on to me.'

'Well perhaps you'll feel better later. Do you need me to go and get some paracetamol or something?'

Camilla took in the baggy grey lounge pants that sat on his slim hips and the soft white surf brand T-shirt that emphasized his broad shoulders and muscular arms. His light brown hair was still sleep-mussed and he needed a shave. He'd never looked better.

'No, I'm fine, really. I probably need a strong coffee and a read. That'll sort me out.'

Tom nodded then planted a kiss on the top of her short damp hair.

'OK, beautiful, as long as you're sure. Think I'll jump in the shower.'

Camilla walked to the door as he turned the shower on, then she turned back, unable to resist admiring his lean frame as he shed his clothes.

Yes, a day lounging around at home with her man sounded pretty perfect, and as for going out later, well they could see how they felt after lunch.

Chapter 8

Allie

Allie was stuffing clothes into the washing machine when she heard footsteps on the stairs. She turned to Chris and he mouthed, *I'll be in the garden.*

This was it then.

Mandy was coming downstairs and Allie would finally find out what had gone wrong.

'Morning, Mum.'

Allie stood up as Mandy entered the kitchen. 'Morning, love. Cup of tea?'

Mandy nodded then shuffled to the table where she sat down and pulled Allie's spare dressing gown around Allie's borrowed pyjamas. Mandy had arrived with just the clothes she was wearing, so Allie had quickly rooted through her things last night to find some garments that would fit her rather slimmed-down daughter.

'Something to eat?' Allie poured milk into two mugs and carried them to the table then went back for the teapot.

'I couldn't face a thing.'

'Are you sure? You need to keep your strength up.'

'Maybe later.'

Allie poured tea into the mugs then passed one to Mandy.

'Thanks.' Mandy raised her puffy red eyes to meet Allie's. 'Sorry, Mum, I didn't mean to be any trouble.'

'You've never been any trouble, love. Just the opposite, in fact. You're so strong and independent that sometimes I wonder if you need me at all. But I'm very proud of you and all that you've achieved.'

Mandy smiled but it didn't reach her eyes. She wrapped her hands around her mug then raised it to her lips and sipped her drink.

'That's good tea.'

'Earl Grey, just how you like it. You do still like it with a splash of skimmed milk don't you?'

'I do. It's good to be home, Mum, even if this isn't the home I grew up in.'

'You always have a place with me. Wherever I am.'

Allie sipped her own tea, wishing her palpitations would stop. Her heart was thrumming so hard, she wondered if it was going to burst through her chest and fly off through the open door. She meant what she'd said; Mandy would always have a place with her but she hoped for Mandy's sake that this man, whoever he was, wouldn't ruin the life Mandy had worked so hard to build. The life that she loved and always spoke about so enthusiastically whenever Allie rang her. Mandy was always getting up early for a meeting or dashing off to another author lunch or book launch. She raved about the latest bestseller to climb the charts — something that author Chris completely understood — and she had dreams of climbing the ladder in publishing; she had such ambitious plans. So many plans.

But now… it seemed as though one man might have ruined all of that.

'I'll be OK, Mum. I just need some time to… compose myself, I guess.'

Mandy moved her neck from side to side as if trying to loosen the knots that had formed there.

'Do you feel ready to talk me about it yet?'

'I do.' Mandy drained her mug. 'But can I have another mug of tea first, please?'

'Of course you can.'

'And actually, perhaps a piece of toast.'

'I have some blueberry muffins that I made yesterday.'

'Your blueberry muffins? Now, Mum, you know I can't resist those.'

Allie set about making more tea then placed a fresh mug and a muffin in front of Mandy. When she sat down again, her stomach was clenched and her mouth dry. She knew she wouldn't be able to eat a morsel until she knew what had happened to her daughter and if it could be sorted, but she'd be glad to see Mandy get some food inside her.

Motherhood was a rollercoaster indeed, and with such love came an open chasm of vulnerability. She'd felt that way the first time she'd held Mandy in her arms and gazed at her perfect tiny features and the soft downy head. The same had happened when she'd held Jordan for the first time too. She'd known she'd do anything for the pair of them, anything at all, and that if anything or anyone ever hurt them, she would become a tigress ready to protect her offspring.

That time had come and she was trying hard not to growl or sharpen her claws…

Chapter 9
Dawn

Dawn pushed the pram up Honey's path then put the brake on and knocked on the door. It was still early and the bedroom curtains were closed, so she hoped she wasn't about to wake Honey and Dane up because she knew Dane needed to rest on his days off. Not that he had many days off according to Honey because he was always doing schoolwork.

Dawn knew how it was to have a busy partner. Rick had worked in the City until last autumn, and most nights, because of the commute as well as long hours, he hadn't got home until after the children had gone to bed. It had been difficult, especially when Dawn got pregnant with Alison. But things had come to a head and Rick had admitted to feeling that he needed to make a big change in his life, and him quitting his City job to work from home was the best decision they had ever made. Yes, money was tighter, especially with three children but they managed and were all happier for it.

She knocked the door again, knowing that now she was here she'd just as well wait until Honey got up, because going back home for what she needed would mean waking her family and then she'd have to explain to Rick what she'd found. The children might overhear and the situation would become a lot worse than it already was.

And it really was bad enough.

Her stomach lurched. She had no idea how she was going to explain it.

The door opened a crack and Dane peered out.

'Good morning, Dane.'

'Dawn?' he opened the door wider and squinted at her. 'Is something wrong?'

'No... no, nothing's wrong,' she replied automatically. 'Well, actually something's wrong but it's nothing to worry about. Well... it is, but I'll deal with it.'

'OK...' He frowned at her and she realized that she sounded absolutely bonkers. Here she was, bright and early on a Bank Holiday Monday, with her newborn baby in her pram, knocking on her friend's door because she didn't want to go home and wake her family.

'Look... could I come in? I promise I won't be long but I need something.'

'You do?'

'Yes. From the shed.'

'From the shed?'

He rubbed his eyes and a wave of sympathy washed over Dawn. It seemed like she actually had woken him up. In fact, he was wearing a pink and purple T-shirt that was riding up his belly and pinching his upper arms.

'Are you wearing one of Honey's T-shirts?' she asked.

He looked down at himself and tugged at the hem but it bounced back up, revealing his flat stomach. Dawn made a point of turning her head and gazing at the Bay tree that stood in a pot next to the door.

'So I am!' He laughed. 'Must've pulled it on by mistake.'
'I'm so sorry if I woke you.'
'It's fine. I wasn't actually sleeping... Anyway, uh, come on in.'

Dane stepped out and helped her lift the pram up the step and into the hallway.

'I'll just call Honey.' He nodded at the stairs.

'Thanks. And... uh... sorry. If I'd had a choice, I wouldn't have disturbed you.'

'No problem.'

Dawn watched as he climbed the stairs two at a time, wondering what it was about him that didn't look right and then she realized. He was wearing white pyjama bottoms with pink hearts printed on them, and they also had to belong to Honey. She winced as she realized that she actually had disturbed them and Dane had grabbed the first items of clothing he could find.

Alison murmured in her pram, so Dawn leant forwards and checked on her. Big grey eyes blinked up at her then the tiny mouth contorted and Alison let out a squawk. She was hungry. Again. Already. Dawn lifted her from the pram then carried her through to the lounge and got comfy on the sofa. She knew Honey wouldn't mind and it would be better than subjecting Honey and Dane to Alison's full dawn chorus of *I'm starving, mother, feed me quick!*

As Alison fed, Dawn relaxed on the comfortable old sofa and gazed at her surroundings. Honey had a lovely home and although a lot of the furniture had belonged to her aunt, and she'd kept it when she'd inherited the cottage, she had also made it her own. Honey was a talented artist who also made sculptures and other crafts, and she'd made Alison a pretty unicorn ornament to celebrate her arrival. It was then that Camilla had recognized the design of the unicorn and they'd found out that Honey was, in fact, behind Purple Hen designs. She'd been quiet about it in her typically unassuming and modest way. However, she'd then admitted that she was doing quite well and had more orders coming in than she could keep up with. Camilla had agreed to take over her accounts to free up some of her time and Dawn had been thinking that once Alison was a bit older, she might be able to help out too, even if it was just driving deliveries around for Honey.

It was an idea for the future anyway, and Dawn wasn't in any rush to see her youngest daughter grow up. She knew how quickly they became independent and she wanted to make the most of having Alison as a baby, because she didn't think they'd try for another. Three children kept them busy enough. As well as the guinea pigs, of course.

'Hello, Dawnie.'

Honey entered the room, her face bright with youth and happiness and her pretty bobbed hair – in shades of blue, pink, purple and silver – pushed behind her ears. The tiny stud in her nose twinkled in the light as she came to sit by Dawn.

'Hi Honey, so sorry to wake you. I was hoping to get in and out quickly but Alison had other ideas.'

'Awww, is she feeding?' Honey sat next to Dawn and gazed at the baby.

'Yes. She's always feeding! My boobs are like balloons because I have so much milk. I saw the health visitor on Friday and she said I have enough milk for five babies and a rice pudding.'

Honey wrinkled her nose. 'Not sure I'd fancy a breast milk rice pudding.'

'Me either, but she did make me giggle.'

'Is everything all right though?' Honey's expression

changed to one of concern. 'I mean… not that it's not great to see you but I'm a bit surprised to see you so early.'

'I know and I'm sorry. Poor Dane seemed shocked.'

Honey nodded. 'I think he was more embarrassed about the fact that he only realized he'd pulled my pyjamas on when he was talking to you. We're both half asleep.'

'Did he? I hardly noticed.' Dawn giggled. 'Pink suits him anyway.'

'Just don't tell the kids at school, whatever you do.'

'My lips are sealed.'

'Do you want a cuppa?'

'I will do, if you don't mind, but first let me tell you what I need and why.'

'That sounds ominous.'

'It's pretty awful and it's something that needs sorting before someone else sees it. Otherwise, it could cause a lot of distress.'

Dawn swallowed as she thought about what she'd seen and how it had turned her stomach. Goodness only knew the impact it could have on those she cared about if she didn't get it cleaned up as soon as possible.

∽

Dawn closed Honey's door behind her and set off back in the direction of her home. After she fed, burped and changed Alison, she'd settled her back in her pram and reassured Honey that Alison would likely sleep for forty-five minutes to an hour. That should give her enough time to do what she needed to do. Dane and Honey had offered to go and deal with the matter but Dawn had declined their help. She'd seen the terrible thing and wanted as few people as possible to see it too. That's what friends were for; sparing one another from upsetting times, as far as was possible anyway.

Honey had seemed nervous at the prospect of looking after Alison, but Dawn had faith in her friend and her ability to care for her daughter. Besides, she wouldn't be long...

When she reached the spot where she'd come across the awful sight, she looked around. It was still early and thankfully quiet, so she should be able to deal with this before anyone else saw it. She pulled the black bin bag Honey had given her from her pocket and shook it out then walked over to the grass and peered around.

Ah... there it was...

Her stomach churned. She could, of course, go and get Rick, but that would defeat the whole purpose of her going to Honey's and waking her and Dane up, so she had to do this herself.

She placed the bag on the ground, edged the spade closer to the black shape, then slid it underneath. It was heavier than she'd anticipated — having only flicked it a small distance earlier on — and when she went to put it inside the black bag, it stuck to the spade, so she had to shake the spade over the bag, all the time trying not to look too closely at what she was doing.

Object bagged — and she had to think of it as an object or she'd get too upset — she tied the handles at the top, wiped the spade on the grass then set off towards Honey's again. But when she got there, she carried on walking. She wasn't taking this to Honey's, she was heading for Tom's surgery. After all, if anyone would know what to do about this, or with this, it would be Tom.

Chapter 10
Camilla

Camilla lowered her book.

'Was that the door?' she asked Tom.

He lowered his book and frowned. They'd just settled for some reading time and now it seemed that it was about to be disturbed.

'Could be an emergency callout.' He grimaced.

'I knew a whole day of relaxing together was too good to be true.'

Camilla accepted his kiss then watched as he left the room and went to the door. When he returned, Dawn was with him. She was pale, her green eyes wide in her pretty face. Her dark hair was pushed behind her ears and she was dressed as though she was about to go for a run.

Camilla stood up.

'God, Dawnie, what's wrong?'

Dawn frowned and Camilla realized she was carrying a black bag and a spade.

'What've you been doing? Clearing up dog poop?'

'No... not exactly. More like road kill.'

'Road kill? Have you gone mad? Get it out of here.' Camilla waved her hands at her sister.

'Actually, I was hoping Tom would take a look at it.'

'You want him to look at a dead animal? Bloody hell, Dawn, it's Bank Holiday Monday and we're trying to chill out together.' She remembered herself. 'And where's Alison?'

Camilla had read about mothers suffering from post-natal issues and acting strangely, walking off and leaving their babies when something distracted them. But picking up road kill? That, she hadn't read about.

'I think that it's...' Dawn bit her lip and Camilla saw that she was actually quite distressed.

'That it's what?'

'I think it's Ebony.'

Camilla's hand shot to her mouth and she met Tom's eyes.

Ebony was one of Allie's beloved cats and she'd be devastated if anything happened to them.

'Let's take it through to the surgery and I can have a look.' Tom took the bag from Dawn then raised it higher as HP came to have a sniff. 'No, HP, nothing in here for you, buddy.'

Dawn turned to Camilla. 'Alison's fine. I left her with Honey after I borrowed the bag and spade.'

'Why didn't you get Rick to do it?'

'He's still in bed. As are the children. I was taking Alison for an early morning stroll to try to get some fresh air and hopefully to make her sleep this morning so I could spend some time with Laura and James, but at the end of our road, I found this cat.'

'Oh, Dawn, that's so sad. And poor Allie. She has

enough on her plate right now, what with Mandy turning up in such a state.'

'Exactly.'

They followed Tom out of the door and around to the vet surgery that was attached to his cottage. Inside, it was cool and dark, the light blue vertical blinds still drawn. The familiar scents of cleaning fluid and animals hung heavy in the air and Camilla's stomach rolled. The surgery was kept spotlessly clean, but the smells could never be fully erased. This was a place where animals were treated and cured. A place where they were born. And a place where, sometimes, they said their final goodbyes to the owners who had loved them.

Tom turned on the lights then went through to the consultation room and placed the bag on the examination table.

'Do you two want to wait outside?'

'No, it's OK. I need to know if it's Ebony.'

Dawn stepped closer to the table but Camilla stayed by the door. The smells and the thought that her friend's cat might be in the bag were making her feel a bit funny.

Tom undid the knotted handles then gently opened the bag and exposed the contents.

Dawn gasped, Tom sighed and Camilla threw up all over the floor.

Chapter 11

Honey

'You don't have to watch her every second you know.' Dane nudged Honey as she stood next to Alison's pram.

She looked up and found him smiling at her.

'I know. I'm just afraid she might wake up and panic.'

'If she does and she sees you staring at her with that goofy smile on your face, she probably will panic.'

Honey touched her mouth. 'Was I goofy?'

He nodded. 'And very, very cute.' He reached out and stroked her hair then ran his fingers down her cheek and her neck until his big hand rested on her shoulder.

'She's just perfect, isn't she?'

He nodded. 'And so are you.'

'I'll get bigheaded if you keep saying such nice things.'

'You deserve to have nice things said to you.' He took her hands. 'Are you OK though?'

'Why wouldn't I be?'

'Well... you know...' He nodded at the pram. 'Having a baby here.'

'Oh…' She chewed her bottom lip. 'I can see why you'd wonder but yes, I'm actually really good.'

She'd recently told Dane all about her past and a miscarriage she'd suffered when she was younger. It had resulted in an infection that meant she didn't know if she'd be able to have children. She'd thought it might put Dane off her, especially as she'd felt to blame for the miscarriage for such a long time, but he had been very understanding, kind and reassuring. He'd told her that he was in no rush to have a family and as long as she wasn't either, then they should be happy getting to know each other and enjoying their time together, and that if one day they wanted to try for a baby, they would deal with any issues then.

'It's lovely having little Alison here and I don't feel under any pressure because no one's watching me. Well, you are but… you know what I mean.'

'I do.' He kissed her softly. 'So you carry on watching her and I'll go and release the hens, shall I?'

'You can if you want. Do you know what to do?'

'I think I can manage a few chickens, Honey. I mean… I'm not exactly going to struggle am I?' He flexed his muscles like some sort of bodybuilder and Honey laughed. She knew he was just teasing.

'You look like you need the toilet when you do that.'

'That's how they do it at the gym. It's the *I'm constipated from all the protein shakes* face.'

'Urgh! OK, you go and get the eggs. But be careful.'

'I will.'

He left her standing there in her lounge, where Dawn had parked the pram, watching the sleeping baby. Ten minutes passed and Dane still hadn't returned.

'You know… I think I need to see how he's getting on,

Alison. Some of my girls can be a bit temperamental, so let's go check up on him shall we?'

She took the brake off then pushed Alison through to the kitchen before clicking the brake on again. What she saw when she looked out of the window made her laugh out loud. Dane needed rescuing already!

'Dane? Are you OK?' she called from the back door. There was no answer, so she gave Alison a quick glance to check she was still sleeping, then hurried out into the garden.

Dane was standing in the chicken enclosure, his hands pressed to his chest, as her chickens bobbed around him. She ran through their names to check that they were all there: Princess Lay-a, Hen-solo, Cluck Rogers, Albert Eggstein, Mary Poopins, Maid Marihen, and Tyrannosaurus Pecks.

Where was...

'Honey!' Dane's voice was strangled as he muttered it through gritted teeth.

'Yes?' She reached the enclosure.

'It... she, rather, keeps coming at me every time I move and pecking my toes.'

'Why have you got flip flops on?'

He shrugged his broad shoulders. 'I thought it would be OK and I haven't moved my wellies in yet.'

'Come on, it's OK... you can get out of there. Just move slowly.'

He lifted his left leg as if he was moving in slow motion and an angry squawk pierced the air, then Henifer Aniston came hurrying around from behind the henhouse. Her head bobbed furiously and she pounced at Dane, pecking at his legs and making him hop from foot to foot as he cried out, then she ran off to assume her hiding position again.

'Oh Dane, I don't think Henifer Aniston likes you.'

'No kidding?' His eyes were wide and he held himself stiffly, as if he was terrified to move again. 'She's like a sniper. Every time I try to leave, she strikes.'

'Uh... right... I know, I'll distract her with some food and you can make your escape.'

'Please be quick!'

Honey went back to the house to fetch some pellets and giggled softly to herself. Big burly Dane, a man who'd been injured in rugby games, a man who'd been through the horrendous goldfish bowl interviews that teachers were subjected to now, and emerged unscathed, was being bullied by a little brown hen. However, Honey knew that Henifer Aniston could be quite territorial and surprisingly fierce when she wanted to be. It must be the Hollywood diva in her.

Honey grabbed the bag of pellets, checked on Alison again, then hurried back out to the garden to rescue the man she loved.

Chapter 12

Allie

Muffin and tea consumed, Mandy had a bit more colour in her cheeks.

'OK, love?' Allie stroked Mandy's hair back from her face in the way she used to when her daughter was a little girl. At least back then, she'd been able to protect Mandy, but now, it was impossible to do so in the same way.

'Yes, that was good, thanks, Mum.'

Allie nodded and took Mandy's plate and mug to the dishwasher.

'Mum?'

'Yes.'

'Am I a bad person?'

'Oh god, no. Of course you're not. Why'd you ask that?'

Mandy crumpled the tissue she'd been holding, passing it from one hand to the other. Allie noted the crimson nail polish on Mandy's nails that matched that on her toenails. The colour would have been perfect with the beautiful ball gown she'd been wearing when she'd arrived the previous day.

'It's just that… I'm so ashamed of myself.'

'Why, love?' Allie sat down next to Mandy and braced herself.

'Because of what happened.'

Allie nodded, not wanting to interrupt Mandy now she'd finally started to talk.

'See… I fell in love with him. With Michael Bloom.'

'Michael Bloom?'

Mandy nodded. 'He's in publishing too. He's a bit older than me.'

'How old?'

'Thirty-three.'

Allie nodded. Nine years or so but what did that matter? Love didn't always care about age.

'He seemed so knowledgeable about the business, so suave and sophisticated.'

Allie swallowed hard, she had a feeling she knew where this was going.

'We met through work and he asked me out. We dated… he'd come to mine but I never went to his. He said he shared his flat with a group of guys, some of whom were doctors and who worked shifts, so it was unfair to take company back. I believed him. That is… I wanted to believe him but I'm not sure I ever really did. Not fully. Something was niggling at the back of my mind.'

'Sometimes we kid ourselves because we want to.'

Mandy nodded. 'Like you did with Dad?'

'What?' Allie's heart plummeted. She'd thought she'd kept Roger's infidelity from her children. When he'd died in the car crash, she hadn't seen the point in hurting them further. Why make them suffer for his behaviour? She'd done her best to maintain their perception of him as a good husband and father.

'I know you tried to protect us, Mum, but things emerged. I put two and two together and... well... he did what he did.'

'But he loved you and Jordan, Mandy. He loved you both so much.'

'I know. I also think he loved you too... as much as he could love anyone. However, he's gone, so we'll never know exactly why he did what he did, will we?'

Allie shook her head. 'I'm sorry, love.'

'Don't be sorry. You're the best mum we could wish for.' Mandy squeezed her hand. 'But Michael did know what he was doing. He took advantage of my naivety; my desire for him – and it was so powerful, Mum, I'd never felt anything like it before – and he played me. I would've done anything for him.'

'Was he... married?'

Mandy nodded. 'With three young children.'

A clattering came from outside and Chris popped his head around the back door. 'Sorry, dropped the watering can.' Then his head disappeared from view again.

'How did you find out?'

'At the party. He'd tried to encourage me not to go, said it would be full of stuffy types and that he thought I'd be better off staying home.'

'He did what?'

'I know, right? Besides which, it was a really big event and everyone who's anyone was going. I didn't want to miss it. Of course, him trying to persuade me not to go raised my suspicions even higher. He said he wasn't going and that he'd come round to mine. I'd already decided to go though, because I'd had enough of him breaking dates, cancelling weekend plans and enough of crying in front of Saturday night TV.'

'Oh Mandy, you should have come home sooner.'

'I needed to live my life, Mum, and I couldn't keep coming home because I was sad about my boyfriend. If that's what he ever actually was.'

'Of course not.' Allie felt her lips turn upwards a fraction. She was so damned proud of her daughter.

'Anyway, I called his bluff and told him I wouldn't go. But I did. I bought a beautiful dress, had my hair and nails done and strolled into that hotel with a smile on my face and my head held high. It started as an amazing evening and it was wonderful to see so many of our authors receiving awards for their incredible sales and for their achievements. The champagne flowed and I was having fun. Until he walked in with a woman on his arm.'

'His wife?'

Mandy stared at her hands as they fidgeted in her lap, pulling the tissue apart.

'She was so beautiful. Slim and elegant with dark brown hair that fell to her shoulders and big brown eyes. She looked like she took really good care of herself, even with young children. I felt so bad, really guilty as they circulated and she hung on his every word, quite obviously adoring him.'

'It's often the way.'

'I was disgusted with myself and with him and I knew I couldn't stay and watch them, so I told my colleagues I had a migraine coming then I grabbed my things and headed for the door.'

Allie took Mandy's left hand and held it tight. The thought of her baby girl enduring such heartache and humiliation was unbearable and she wished she could go back in time and stop her daughter getting hurt. But that wasn't possible and Mandy had to live her life her way.

'I'd reached the door when I felt a hand on my shoulder. I turned around and found her... his wife... staring at me. She didn't look angry, just sad, and then she said... she said... 'Michael might play around away from home but you're not the first and you won't be the last.' She said that he loved her and the children and he loved her money. That he'd never leave her.'

'How did she knew about you?'

'Apparently he wasn't as good at covering his tracks as he thought. But it was weird because she was so cold, like a robot as she spoke. Almost as if she'd rehearsed the words or said them before.'

'Oh dear.'

'She also said that as long as I didn't force the issue with him, I was welcome to carry on seeing him. But there's no way I would after finding out he was married. What would that make me, Mum? I'm not a cheat and a bitch and I would never want to hurt another woman or her children.'

'I know, love, I know.'

'I told her I had no idea he was married and that if I had, I'd never have had anything to do with him. She just stared at me in that same detached away then told me she pitied me and walked away. Right into his arms. You know... the worst thing was that he watched her speaking to me from across the room, then when she rejoined him, he met my eyes and gave a small nod. As if he thought we would carry on now with his wife's approval. I ran outside and threw up all down the hotel steps then grabbed a taxi to the station.'

'What a complete shit!' Allie muttered.

Mandy gave a wry laugh.

'Yeah... but I guess I had a lucky escape. Imagine being with a man who loved your money more than you. I just feel sorry for her and their children.'

'Children grow up and where will they be then? That poor woman.'

'She knows what she's got though, doesn't she? I didn't know what I was getting into. I made a big mistake and it's one I certainly won't be repeating.'

'What about your job? I know how much you love it.'

'I don't have to see him very often and he was talking about a promotion to a different department anyway. He said he'd delayed it so he could still see me but I suspect he'll be keen to avoid me now.'

'Oh, sweetheart, I'm sorry you went through all that.'

'Life eh, Mum. And you know what… Speaking to you about it and being back in Heatherlea really helps.'

'Do you need to ring work to tell them you're sick?'

'Not today as it's a Bank Holiday but I'll ring in tomorrow and say I'll be back on Wednesday, perhaps even next week. I need to catch my breath and I'm owed some holiday.'

'You can stay here as long as you like.'

'Thanks, Mum.'

'Don't thank me. That's what I'm here for.'

As Allie hugged her daughter tight, she sent out a silent thank you that Mandy was a survivor, that she was strong enough to pull through this. Better now than later when she could have children of her own. Better that she could walk away from this man and his deceit and start again.

Chris appeared in the back doorway. 'Did you hear knocking? I think someone's at the front door.'

He pulled off his gardening gloves and strode through the kitchen and into the hallway. Allie and Mandy listened as he opened the door.

When he returned to the kitchen, Dawn and Camilla were with him.

'Hi ladies.' Allie stood up. 'To what do we owe this pleasure?'

They both looked at Mandy then back at Allie.

'What is it? You both look like you woke up to find someone stole the milk from your doorsteps.'

'Everything OK?' Dawn asked, as she nodded in Mandy's direction.

'I'm fine thank you, Dawn. Well, I will be anyway.' Mandy smiled.

'Ah... good. Glad to hear it. Could... uh... could Camilla and I have a word, Allie?'

'Of course. Do you want a cuppa?'

Camilla shook her head. 'No, thanks. Better to get this over and done with.'

Allie placed the kettle back on its stand and looked at her friends. 'You're scaring me now. What on earth is wrong?'

'It's... it's Ebony.'

'Ebony?'

'Yes...' Dawn released a long sigh then rubbed her cheeks. You see... this morning I... I found something terrible. And I'm so sorry to have to deliver this bad news now but...'

Dawn's jaw dropped and she stared at the open back door where the sunlight was warming the tiles of the kitchen floor.

'Oh. My. God!'

Chapter 13

Dawn

'I don't believe it.' Dawn's hand flew out and tapped Camilla's arm.

'Ouch! Careful, Dawn!'

'But it's...'

'I can bloody well see what it is. It's Ebony. And she's here.'

'Of course it's Ebony.' Allie frowned. 'Where else would she be?'

'At Tom's surgery...' Camilla offered, her raised eyebrows suggesting she didn't believe that for one minute.

'What would she be doing there?' Allie asked.

'Oh no!' Dawn covered her mouth. 'I've only gone and picked up someone else's cat.'

'Indeed you have.' Camilla folded her arms across her chest and shook her head. 'Why didn't you check properly?'

'Tom checked the cat over and he couldn't tell that it wasn't Ebony. Besides which, you saw the state it was in; there wasn't much to check. Although...' Dawn turned to her sister. 'It seems there was enough to make you vomit. I never thought of you as being squeamish.'

Allie was staring at them, her eyes wide, and Mandy was watching their exchange with a matching bemused expression.

'Camilla was sick when Tom got the cat out of the bag.'

'The bag?'

'Yes, see, I found a squashed cat this morning and I went to Honey's for a spade and a bag then I scooped it up and took it to the vet.'

'Why?' Allie was shaking her head.

'I thought it was Ebony and I didn't want you to see her like that.'

'Oh, Dawn, you softy.'

'She is a softy.' Camilla nodded.

'You could have called me, Dawn. I would've come to get her.' Chris went to the kettle and switched it on.

'I couldn't do that. You had Mandy here and I knew you'd be busy.'

'Well thank goodness it isn't Ebony.' Allie sighed. 'I don't think I could have coped with that on top of everything else.'

They all looked at the black cat currently lying on her side in the patch of sunlight, legs stretched out and tail gently flicking back and forth. As if on cue, Ebony started purring.

'Yes, thank goodness.' Dawn nodded.

'So whose cat is it?' Mandy asked.

'No idea but I'd better go back and let Tom know.' Camilla licked her lips. 'Could I have a glass of water first though, please? I have such a dry mouth this morning.'

'Of course.'

Allie filled a glass from the tap and handed it to Camilla.

'I'd better get going too. I left Alison with Honey.' Dawn pushed her hair back from her forehead.

'Why? Where's Rick?' Allie asked.

'It's a long story but basically he's still in bed, as are Laura and James. Anyway, I'll catch up with you later.'

Camilla handed Allie the empty glass then they walked to the front door and Allie waved them off.

'I can't believe that just happened.' Dawn tutted as they walked along the street.

'Me either. But you did the right thing.'

'I guess so. You go and tell Tom and I'll let Honey and Dane know about the mistaken identity of the black cat.'

'The cat you let out of the bag?'

'Ha! Ha!'

'OK, ring you later.'

'Bye!'

Dawn headed back towards Honey's cottage, feeling a lot lighter than she had done half an hour ago. So she'd cleaned up someone's dead cat but thankfully it wasn't Ebony. So much for good deeds. Although it was very sad that a poor cat had suffered that awful fate. Still, it would make an interesting anecdote to share with Rick when she got home, that she went around picking up squashed cats.

The positive thing about the morning though, was that Mandy had looked all right when they'd walked into Allie's kitchen, so hopefully her situation wasn't as bad as it had seemed yesterday.

Things were looking up.

Weren't they?

Chapter 14
Camilla

Camilla was walking back to the surgery, running the events of that morning through her head, when she stopped suddenly. Dawn was right; she wasn't usually that squeamish. But something about the situation: the smell and the thought of what was in the bag and how upset Allie would be had combined to make her head spin, causing her to throw up.

She decided to take a quick detour and pop into her cottage, as she wanted to use some mouthwash and Tom hadn't had any at his cottage. She let herself in and closed the door behind her then went straight up the stairs to the bathroom. She filled the cap of the bottle with peppermint mouthwash then swilled it around her mouth before spitting it into the sink.

As she placed it back in the cabinet, something caught her eye. She reached for the small cardboard packet full of small blue pills and turned it over in her hands.

Then she did a quick calculation.

She'd been so busy lately with Tom, work and caught up with Dawn and her new baby, as well as her recently reunited parents, that she'd not been as careful with her contraceptive pill as she used to be. She'd taken it at different times of the day, sometimes the following day if she'd stayed the night at Tom's and forgotten to take the pills with her, but she'd just assumed she'd be fine.

Hadn't she?

Or had she been deliberately lax?

She shook her head at her reflection. Camilla was sensible, reliable, a career woman.

Her reflection stared back at her: huge green eyes, porcelain skin and short dark hair. There was something different about her eyes, for sure. They'd always been large but now they seemed positively luminescent, even though, apart from that, she didn't look well; a bit peaky, as her mum would say.

She couldn't be… could she?

There was that one night when she was at the end of her packet and she'd left it at home, and the next day, she thought it wouldn't matter as it was the end of the three weeks and she was due her pill-free week. She needed to speak to Dawn, see what her sister thought of the situation. Dawn had experience in these matters, having been pregnant three times, the third pregnancy being an accident, if a very happy one. If Camilla was pregnant, then what a pair of sisters they were, getting caught out and at their ages!

She shrugged. What would be would be. And it was highly likely that this was all in her mind and her period would arrive tomorrow. She padded down the stairs and back out into the sunlight then made her way to Dawn's. When she got there she knocked gently on the door. No answer.

Wasn't Dawn back yet then? She had needed to collect Alison from Honey's, so perhaps she'd stopped for a cuppa.

She heard a noise inside then Rick appeared at the door in a pair of blue and grey striped pyjama bottoms with a white T-shirt on top. He frowned at her then ran a hand over his face.

'Morning, Camilla. I don't suppose you've seen my wife, have you?'

'I have actually. Can I come in.'

'Of course.' He stepped back. 'Is she all right?'

'She's fine.'

'OK... Cup of tea?'

'Please.'

She followed him through to the kitchen and took a chair at the kitchen table while he filled the kettle and switched it on.

'Dawn went out for walk earlier with Alison. She said she didn't want to wake you and hoped the fresh air might help the baby sleep this morning.'

'Ah... thought it might be something like that.' Rick nodded. 'Where is she now though and how did you bump into her? You doing the walk of shame or something?'

'What?'

'You know; sneaking home early in the morning in the clothes you wore the night before.'

'Ha! No, not at all. Dawn came to Tom's because she'd found a dead cat and thought it was Ebony.'

'Allie's cat?'

'Yes.'

'Was it?'

'No, thank goodness. Allie would have been devastated. We went to tell Allie that we thought it was Ebony and the cat was sunning herself in the kitchen.'

'So Tom now has a dead cat and you don't know whose it is?'

Camilla nodded, swallowing hard as that strange feeling crawled over her again at the thought of that poor squashed creature.

'Fancy a bacon sandwich?' Rick asked.

Camilla shook her head. 'No. No thanks. Got to... use the bathroom.'

'The downstairs loo's not working. James broke the flush. Better go upstairs!'

She rushed to the stairs, hurried up them then locked herself in the cool white space that smelt of lemons and toothpaste. She knelt in front of the toilet and took some slow breaths until the churning stopped then she sat back on her haunches and looked around. Her sister's bathroom was a perfect family space with its clean white bathroom suite and large walk-in shower cubicle. Along the side of the bath, Laura and James's toys were lined up, from toy dinosaurs to a Barbie wearing a bright pink swimming costume. Along the windowsill were bottles of baby shampoo, bubble bath and conditioner. The lemon aroma was the result of the bathroom cleaner that sat high up on top of the cabinet, out of the children's reach.

Camilla wondered what she would be like as a mother, if it ever happened for her. She'd tried to imagine it in the past but it just wasn't a role she could picture herself in easily. She'd probably forget to put the bleach and spray up out of reach or use normal shampoo on the baby and make its eyes sting. Some women, like Dawn, were natural mothers but Camilla hadn't experienced that powerful maternal instinct and didn't think she'd know what to do.

And what on earth would Tom think?

She shuddered, then stood up and opened the bathroom cabinet, hoping she'd find some paracetamol as her head had started to throb.

She moved a few things and came across a long thin white box with blue writing. She pulled it out and read the side then she shook her head. There was no need for that. Overreaction or what? But her hand just wouldn't let go of the box, so in the end she closed the cupboard and leant against the sink, staring at the blue writing as if it could tell her what to do for the best.

This would clear things up, wouldn't it? If she used one of these, she'd know one way or the other for sure. She was about to open the box when there was a frantic hammering at the door.

'Mummy? Is that you?'

'No, it's me.'

'Auntie Camilla?'

'Yes.'

'Oh. What're you doing here?'

'I came to visit.' Camilla stuffed the box into the back of the waistband of her jeans then tucked her shirt over it.

'Where's Mummy?'

'Gone for a walk. She won't be long.'

'Auntie Camilla?'

'Yes?'

'Can I use the toilet? I'm bursting.'

'Oh! Of course.'

Camilla opened the door and smiled at her pretty niece, but the smell of bacon cooking hit her full force so she turned on her heel and rushed to the toilet, emptying her stomach for the second time that morning.

Chapter 15
Honey

'It's not funny you two.' Dane frowned at Honey and Dawn as they giggled together at the kitchen table. Dawn had arrived just after Honey had succeeded in rescuing Dane from Henifer Aniston. He'd been visibly shaken at his encounter with the bossy hen.

'Oh Dane but it was very amusing. You have to see the funny side of it.' Honey wiped her eyes on her sleeve then sipped her tea.

'For you maybe but you didn't have your legs and toes pecked.'

'He really is henpecked and he's only just moved in.' Dawn snorted and Honey joined her in a fresh fit of giggles.

'Well I think it's roast chicken for dinner.' Dane folded his arms across his broad chest.

'Don't you dare. None of my hens are ever going to end up on a plate.' Honey nudged him. 'They're my girls and anyway, you wait and see. They'll come round and warm to you.'

'When he comes out of his shell a bit.' Dawn's eyes widened at her own joke.

'And conquers his fear of the poultrygeist.'

'Right that's it! I'm going to make some more tea.' Dane stood up then picked up their mugs. 'Actually... I've just thought of one.'

'Go on then...' Honey watched him. 'If you're up to it after your hen-counter.'

Dane's lips twitched. 'Right, here goes... How do baby chickens dance?'

Honey and Dawn shook their heads.

'Chick-to-chick.' He smiled. 'Actually, Honey, after that attack, I think I need you to do a thorough eggsamination of me.'

Dawn and Honey laughed until Honey's sides ached.

A murmur from the pram at Dawn's side made her peer into the pram.

'Ah, I'd better get going. I didn't mean to stay this long anyway and Rick's probably up by now.'

'I'll see you out.'

Honey walked Dawn and Alison to the door.

'Hope she sleeps for you today.'

'Yeah, me too. Still, at least Rick's had a lie-in, so he'll be there if I need to grab a nap.'

'I still can't believe you went to all that trouble only to find it wasn't even Ebony.'

'I know, but I couldn't leave the cat there, could I?'

Honey shook her head. 'At least it wasn't Ebony.'

'There is that.'

'What will Tom do with the cat now?'

'Probably cremation, I suppose. If no one claims it. It could well be feral.'

Honey shivered. 'Poor thing.'

'I know.'

'Anyway, thanks for watching Alison.'

'It was a pleasure. She's beautiful.'

Honey closed the door then went back through to the kitchen. Dane was standing at the backdoor peering out into the garden.

'You OK?' She slid her arms around his waist and buried her face in his back, breathing in his wonderful scent and enjoying the feel of his hard body against hers.

'Yeah. As long as you don't think I'm a wimp for being bullied by your chicken.'

He turned in her arms and hugged her back.

'I think you're amazing, Dane.'

His eyes lit up as he smiled at her. 'Well that feeling is mutual.'

'Do you fancy getting out for a bit? Perhaps go to the café?'

'Sure, why not? But first I need that eggsamination you promised me.'

'I promised you one did I?'

He nodded, then pulled her closer.

Chapter 16

Allie

'Right, love, why don't you take a long hot bath?' Allie had loaded the dishwasher and she switched it on. 'Everything's done here and you look like you need to relax.'

'That sounds like a wonderful idea, Mum. What about you? Do you and Chris have plans today?'

'I think Chris wanted to spend some time sorting the garden out but I said I'll spend a few hours at the café. Jordan's opening up but I'd better be there to help him in case we have a lunchtime rush.'

'On a Bank Holiday?'

Allie nodded. 'Might get some people passing through as well as the local regulars. The café has been doing really well.'

'I'm so happy for you, Mum. You know... with how things have worked out with the café and with Chris. He's a keeper.'

'I heard that!' Chris called from outside.

'It was all good.'

'Thank you!'

Allie smiled. To have her daughter and Chris in the same house on a sunny morning was wonderful. It had been a long time since Mandy had been in Heatherlea and Allie hoped that she might stay for a bit. She wanted Mandy to go back to her London and to her career, of course, but not just yet.

'I think I will take that bath.'

'There's some jasmine bubble bath in the cupboard and it smells divine. Help yourself.'

'Thanks, Mum.'

Allie hugged her daughter tight, hoping that Mandy knew how special she was and that one idiotic man wouldn't taint her views of herself and of love. Allie knew how it was to have a man break her heart, but then Chris had come along and helped her to heal. She hoped Mandy would heal too and one day, perhaps learn to trust again.

Chapter 17

Dawn

Dawn reached the end of her street again and slowed down. It had been a busy morning and had certainly turned out differently than she could have imagined. She'd thought to have a nice walk then get back to bed, even to the sofa and grab more sleep, but fate had apparently had other plans for her.

Fate? She shook her head. Sometimes she thought it was fate, sometimes she believed she made her own luck. But that poor cat had certainly not seen the car that had squished it coming.

She swerved to avoid the dark patch where the cat had been, and paused.

What was that sound?

Meowing? Faint but there nonetheless.

She looked around. Nothing on the road or the street. She pushed the brake on the pram down then walked towards the long grass just off the pavement. She moved it aside and peered under the hedge. And her heart broke, because there, in what looked like some kind of nest, were two small kittens.

The mewled pitifully, sending Dawn's maternal instincts soaring. The cat she'd found must have been their mother and they'd lost her. How would they manage? They probably wouldn't. They were moving around but they looked so small and lost. They wanted their mum.

Dawn knew she couldn't leave them there, so she leant forwards and gently picked them both up. They cried out so she tucked them into her loose T-shirt, making a kind of hammock out of the front, then she kicked off the brake on the pram and slowly walked towards home, pushing the pram with one hand with cradling the kittens with the other.

Goodness only knew what Rick would say when he found out what she'd been up to that morning, but some days were like this. Unpredictable. Unexpected. And as far as Dawn was concerned, she had been in the right place at the right time as far as the kittens were concerned.

Outside the front door she pushed down the brake on the pram again then knocked gently, not wanting to have to try to search in her bag for her key.

The door opened and Rick smiled at her. 'Morning walkies, eh? You should have woken me.'

'You were out cold and I wanted you to get more sleep.'

'Well come on in and you can grab a nap while I give the children breakfast.'

'Ok. But, Rick...'

He was already lifting the pram over the front doorstep.

'Yeah?'

'I... I have something to tell you.'

'It's OK,' he said from inside, 'Camilla told me about the cat. Trust you to feel the need to move it.'

'I couldn't exactly leave it there, could I? And how did Camilla tell you?'

'I'm here, Dawnie.'

Camilla came down the stairs just as Dawn stepped inside.

'Oh, hi. What're you? Why did you...'

'I came to ask you something but you weren't back so Rick made me tea.'

'I also offered her breakfast but apparently the thought of my cooking made her sick.'

'You were sick again?' Dawn winced. 'I hope it's not a bug.'

'Yeah, me too.' Camilla's eyes widened and she shook her head a fraction, just enough to let Dawn know that she had something she wanted to speak to her about. 'Why's your T-shirt moving?' Camilla gestured at Dawn's belly.

'That's what I was trying to explain to Rick. On my way back, I heard a noise in the bushes and found these two.' She opened her T-shirt to show her husband and Camilla.

'Oh my goodness!' Camilla lifted one of the tiny kittens and held it to her chest. 'How sweet.'

'You found them where?' Rick asked.

'Under the hedge at the end of the street.'

'Probably feral and crawling with fleas then.' Rick grimaced and Camilla immediately held the kitten away from her body.

'Maybe but I couldn't leave them there. And what if they're not wild and the mother was somebody's pet that went missing?' Dawn asked.

'We'd better take them to Tom so he can check them over,' Rick said. 'They look about seven weeks old, possibly eight.'

'So that means they still need milk, doesn't it?' Dawn smoothed the soft gently domed head of the kitten she was holding.

'I'm no cat expert but possibly.' Rick scratched his head. 'Let me grab a box from the garage for them and we can give Tom a ring.'

Ten minutes later, the kittens were sleeping, curled up together on a soft wool blanket that Rick had tucked into the box. They'd seemed exhausted and she wondered if they'd been up all night waiting for their mother. Rick had taken them through to the kitchen and put the box in the corner away from drafts. Thankfully, they hadn't seemed to have fleas when Rick had checked them over but she knew Tom would need to see them to give them a proper examination.

'Don't disturb them, mind.' Dawn whispered to Laura and James as they sat in front of the box watching the kittens. Her children had come downstairs to find their mother and auntie cradling the orphaned kittens and immediately asked if they could keep them.

Rick had stepped in to say that they were too young to be pets yet and that they weren't to get attached. As if that was going to happen. Dawn was already smitten herself, imagining that the two cats would make a lovely addition to their family. After all, they had the guinea pig family out in the garden, so why not adopt two family cats as well?

'I'll take them back to the surgery, shall I, and see what Tom thinks?' Camilla asked as she peered over Laura and James's heads at the kittens.

'I'll come with you.' Dawn nodded, deciding that she'd just as well be there for that too. 'I need to feed Alison first though.'

'No problem.'

'Dawn, I'll take them and you can stay here and rest,' Rick said.

'Really?' Dawn looked at their three children in turn. 'I would but I'm not sure I'll be able to relax until I know that the kittens are OK. It's so sad that they were orphaned like that.'

Camilla nodded then a sob escaped her and she buried her face in her hands.

'Camilla?' Dawn reached out and squeezed her sister's shoulder. It wasn't like Camilla to show emotion. She'd been a bit softer since she'd got together with Tom, for certain, but bursting into tears?

'It's just... they lost their mum.'

'I know...' Dawn rubbed Camilla's shoulder and made a face at Rick. 'We'll look after them, don't you worry.'

Camilla nodded. 'Sorry. I don't know what's got into me.' She met Dawn's eyes and her cheeks flushed.

Dawn felt her mouth drop open as realization washed over her.

Pale.

Vomiting.

Emotional.

Oh Camilla...

Chapter 18

Camilla

Camilla and Dawn had taken the kittens to the surgery and Tom had checked them over then declared that they seemed fit and well. He'd said he could keep them in for a few days for observation, as they were still a bit young to be away from their mother, and that he had some weaning milk he could make up for them, as well as some kitten food. Camilla had then made her excuses to leave with Dawn, stating that they'd agreed to meet Allie at the café for an hour but she'd promised not to be long.

Truth be told, she needed to be away from Tom while she did what she needed to do. The small box with the blue writing was still tucked into her waistband and she pressed a hand to it, feeling its reassuring presence.

'Camilla, do you want to talk about it?'

'About what?'

Dawn put a hand in front of Camilla to stop her, then glanced around them but the tree-lined street was quiet.

'About the way you've been feeling. The nausea. The

emotional reactions that are not exactly characteristic of you, no offence, sis.'

Camilla met her sister's green eyes and the emotion Dawn had referred to surged within her again.

'Not really.' She bit the inside of her cheek. 'I can't.'

Dawn squeezed her shoulder. 'You can, you know? I love you and I'm here for you.'

Camilla nodded and Dawn pulled her into a hug. She rocked her gently, as she would one of her children and Camilla had to take slow deep breaths to stop herself from crying. Dawn rubbed her back then paused and Camilla realized that her sister had brushed her hand over the box stuffed into the back of her jeans.

'Camilla?'

'Yes?'

'Are you wearing a wire?'

'What?' In spite of her distress, Camilla snorted at the question.

Dawn leant back and smiled at her. 'You know, like on reality TV shows where they have the electronic pack or whatever it is stuffed into their trousers or the back of their dress.'

'It's not a wire and we're not on TV.'

'Thank goodness for that!' Dawn laughed.

Camilla reached under her shirt and pulled out the box, then watched as understanding filled Dawn's face.

'I took it from your bathroom. I was looking for tablets for my headache and I saw this and thought it might be a good idea to try it. Or to do it, or whatever...'

'So you do think you could be...' Dawn let the unfinished question hang in the air.

'I'm not sure. I mean... it's a long shot but I don't feel right and if it's not that then it could be something else.'

'Like what?' Dawn frowned.

'I don't know. Like early menopause or... cancer or some other horrid illness I suppose.'

Dawn shook her head. 'I know you and I've been in your shoes, just about, and I'm pretty certain that you're pregnant.'

'Oh god!' Camilla gasped. 'Don't say that! Don't say those words! I'm not ready for this. I don't think I ever will be.'

'Look, there's no point stressing about it until you know for sure. Worst case scenario, it's some sort of bug that will pass in a few days.'

'That's the worst-case scenario? What's the best case?'

'I'm going to be an auntie!' Dawn hugged her tight and Camilla exhaled shakily. 'This is a good thing, sweetheart. Try not to worry. Now let's go get a drink at the café and you can pee on that stick.'

'OK. Not words I expected to hear today, but I'll try to go with the flow.'

'The flow!' Dawn giggled. 'Yes you need to pop the test stick under the flow. Sorry. This is a serious matter.'

'Indeed it is. But I don't know whether to laugh or cry.'

Camilla let Dawn take her hand and lead her towards her destiny.

Whatever that might be...

Chapter 19

Honey

'MMM. This is so good.' Honey took another bite of the fresh buttery croissant and chewed. Neither of them had fancied eggs following Henifer Aniston's attack.

'We worked up quite an appetite didn't we?' Dane grinned at her across the table that was next to the front window of The Cosy Cottage Café.

'We certainly did, you especially what with all that running away from Henifer Aniston.'

Dane shook his head. 'That wasn't what I meant.'

'I know. I'm teasing you.' Honey reached out and stroked his hand where it rested on the table next to his mug of coffee.

'I'm actually quite upset that she doesn't seem to like me.' Dane licked a finger then dabbed at some croissant crumbs on his plate and put them into his mouth. 'I mean... how are we going to manage if I can't help with the chickens?'

'We'll manage, Dane. I've been taking care of them alone for some time.'

Dane frowned.

'What is it?'

'I don't want you doing everything alone, Honey. We're partners and I want us to share the responsibility of running the home and looking after the animals.'

Honey slid her hand into his. He really was a good man and she felt very lucky to have him in her life.

'I'm sure we'll work it out. Perhaps once Henifer gets to know you, she'll be less... aggressive.'

'I hope so.'

Dane raised her hand and kissed it.

'Breakfast all right?' Allie asked as she appeared at their table.

'Lovely, thanks. The croissants were perfect.'

Allie smiled. 'Good. At least I got something right.'

'What do you mean?' Honey asked.

Allie looked around at the other customers in the café then pulled out a chair and sat down.

'I've tried to help Mandy since she came home in that awful state but I can't help feeling as though I failed her in some way.'

'You haven't failed her.' Honey looked at Allie's hands where they sat on the table, wringing a tea towel between them. 'You're a great mum.'

Allie grimaced. 'I wonder if I am though. Didn't I make her strong enough to deal with whatever life might throw at her? Could I have made her more resilient and less inclined to fall for someone who would shred her confidence? It could be that I didn't compensate for Roger's death enough and that left her needing something, craving something from a man that made her vulnerable.'

Honey shook her head. Allie had briefly filled them in on Mandy's situation when they'd arrived at the café. 'Allie,

Roger's death was not your fault and you have done everything you could to show your children that they are loved and supported. Look at how happy Jordan is. Mandy is just going through what many people do. Lots of us have our hearts broken along the way.'

'I know that's true.' Allie smiled. 'It's hard being a mum. I just want to wrap them up in a soft blanket like I did when they were babies and protect them from the world.'

'Well you can't do that,' Dane said. 'But you are there for them and your love and support is more than a lot of children get from their parents, believe me.'

'He's right, Allie. You can't protect them from life but you can be there to help ease them over the hurdles.'

'Thank you.' Allie stood up. 'You're both very kind. More coffee?'

'That would be lovely.'

Chapter 20
Allie

Allie was trying to focus on making coffees for Honey and Dane but her thoughts were firmly planted at home with her daughter. Mandy would come through this and hopefully go on to have a great life but if Allie had been able to have her way, she'd protect Mandy from any upset at all. That was the difficult thing with parenting; your children grew up and you couldn't protect them from life and love; you had to let them make their own mistakes.

After all, hadn't her own parents worried about her over the years? Her mother had told her that they'd had to bite their tongues hundreds of times to avoid interfering in Allie's life. But when they'd felt compelled to try to advise her, Allie had often brushed their concerns away, convinced that she was following the right path. It was surely natural to rebel against whatever your parents thought was for the best...

She picked up the coffees and was about to take them over to Honey and Dane when the door opened and Dawn and Camilla entered. The sisters were so alike that it sometimes made her do a double take. With their dark hair, pale skin and those clear green eyes, they were like Elizabeth Taylor in her heyday.

'Hi Allie!' Dawn waved but Camilla scanned the café before following her sister over to the counter.

'Hello both. How are you now?'

'Good thanks.' Dawn smiled. 'What about you?'

Allie gave a small shrug. 'We just have to get on with things, don't we? I keep telling myself that Mandy will be fine and hoping I'm right.'

Concern flashed through her when she looked closely at Camilla. Her skin was so pale it was almost translucent.

'Are you all right, Camilla?'

'What? Oh... yes, I'm fine. I just need the loo.'

'You know where it is!' Allie used the well-worn phrase but Camilla just blinked.

'Yes. OK. Uh... I'm going to go to the loo now.'

Dawn rubbed her shoulder. 'You want me to come with you?'

Allie put the coffees back down on the counter. Since when did Camilla need her sister to take her to the toilet?

'No, thanks. It's fine. It'll all be fine.' Camilla nodded then headed for the door that led to the café toilets.

'Is she OK?' Allie asked Dawn.

'Yeah... she's fine. How many times have we all used that word this morning?' She shook her head. 'Camilla is just a bit tired I think.' Dawn's cheeks coloured and Allie wondered what was going on. If the sisters had a secret then that was fine, but they were both acting strangely and she felt sure there must be more to it than the whole dead cat debacle of that morning.

'Do you want a coffee?' Allie asked.

'Better not as I'm breastfeeding, and I don't want to

mess with Alison's sleep via a milky caffeine infusion if I can help it. I'll have a glass of something cold, though, please.'

'What about Camilla? Shall I make her a drink?'

'Uh… yes please, she'll have a cold drink too.'

'Any preference?'

'Surprise us. Shall I take those to the customers?'

'They're for Honey and Dane.'

'OK, I'll pop them over then come back for ours.'

'Thanks.'

Allie went through to the kitchen and opened the large fridge then brought out a bottle of sparkling elderflower juice. She'd make the sisters a refreshing mocktail and hopefully find out what was going on with them, but only if they wanted her to know.

Chapter 21

Dawn

'There you are. Two coffees.'

Dawn set the mugs down on the table in front of Dane and Honey.

'Thanks, Dawn. How are you feeling after your busy morning?'

'Ah you know... Relieved that Ebony was fine but a bit sad that those kittens ended up without their mum.' Dawn had sent a text to Honey to tell her about the kittens, hoping it was something positive to come out of the sad situation with the squashed cat.

'Yes so sad.' Honey shook her head. 'Hope they find homes.'

'I'm sure they will. They are so cute! Tom's keeping them in for a while but once he's run some blood tests and fed them up a bit, they'll be looking for homes.' Dawn grinned. 'I'm hoping Rick will let me keep them to be honest. I don't want to split them up and they're just adorable. The children would love them.'

'Well if Rick doesn't agree, let us know and I'm sure we

can come up with a plan.' Dane smiled as he took Honey's hand.

'Oh we can, can we?' Honey tilted her head. 'And what will that be?'

'I've always wanted to have a cat.'

'Really?'

He nodded. 'But if Dawn takes the kittens on, then perhaps we should visit a rehoming centre.'

'That sounds like a rather big commitment to me, Mr Ackerman.' Honey waggled her eyebrows.

'I'm up for that.'

Honey blushed with pleasure then met Dawn's eyes and smiled.

'I'll keep you posted on them.' Dawn glanced over at the counter. 'I think our drinks are ready.'

'Come join us if you want?' Honey patted the chair next to her.

'What and cramp your style? Ruin your romantic brunch, or is it lunch now... for two?'

'It's fine, really.' Dane gestured at the empty chairs. 'Please join us.'

'Back in a bit then.'

Dawn went over to the counter and accepted the drinks from Allie.

'Ooh! These look nice. What are they?'

'Mocktails. Sparkling elderflower, lemon juice and some fresh mint. Nice and refreshing.'

'Sounds yummy.'

'Is Camilla still in the toilet?'

Dawn nodded.

'She must have quite an upset stomach...'

Dawn frowned. 'I'd better go and check on her.'

She walked towards the toilets but when she reached the door, it opened and Camilla came out. Her skin was waxy and dark shadows sat beneath her eyes like bruises. She stopped when she saw Dawn and her bottom lip wobbled.

'Oh god… try to be strong, sweetheart.' Dawn muttered under her breath. She took hold of Camilla's hand and led her to the counter. 'Look at these lovely drinks Allie made for us. Shall we go and sit down and enjoy them?' She was aware that her voice sounded too bright, that her smile was too wide.

'OK.'

Just then, the door opened and Tom entered, turning to close the door behind him. Camilla gasped then shot behind the counter and through the door that led to the kitchen, while Allie and Dawn stared at each other, their mouths gaping and their eyes wide.

Dawn knew what must be wrong but Allie didn't, so Camilla's behaviour must seem very strange to their friend.

Chapter 22
Camilla

In the kitchen, Camilla scanned the room for somewhere to hide the white stick that she'd tucked into the waistband of her jeans. She'd followed the directions and peed on the stick then been unable to look at it. She couldn't deal with this now, so she'd have to find out what the result was later. Although the directions said that you had to read the results as soon as possible for accuracy.

Accuracy...

Damn that word. As an accountant she usually loved accuracy but today she felt differently. If she'd been accurate with taking her pill and so on, then she wouldn't even be worried at all now.

She pulled the stick out of her waistband and held it out.

Her hand was shaking.

Turning the stick over slowly, she brought it closer to her face.

She took a deep breath.

Here goes...

'Oh...' She stared at the two blue lines sitting side by side. 'Oh... dear.'

Her legs were trembling so badly, she thought she'd keel over if she didn't take a seat soon. But she also couldn't take the stick with her so she needed somewhere to leave it.

Voices in the café carried through and she recognized Tom's.

What if he came looking for her? She scanned the kitchen and her gaze fell on Allie's bag tucked under the island in one of the baskets. That would do for now! She dropped the test into it and tucked it back in the basket. She'd explain to Allie when she got five minutes, but for now she'd better go back out and act normal. Well, as normal as she could do knowing that Tom's baby was growing in her womb.

Baby?
Womb?
GAAAAHHHH!

What would he think? Would he hate her and blame her for getting pregnant? Would he be horrified? Shocked? Was there a chance that he'd be happy about it all?

Nausea swirled in her belly and she took a few slow deep breaths. She could remember hearing that morning sickness was a sign of a strong pregnancy, but the idea of feeling like this for any length of time scared her. She could barely think straight let alone carry on as normal. But she'd have to until she decided what to do or Tom would know something was up.

She pinched her cheeks, licked her lips then pushed her shoulders back and headed for the door. She was a strong and confident woman and she'd dealt with plenty of difficult situations over the years.

She could deal with this.
Of course she could.
Couldn't she?

Chapter 23

Honey

Over Dane's shoulder, Honey had seen Camilla shoot into the kitchen when Tom entered the café, as well as Dawn and Allie's bewildered faces. There was definitely something strange going on and she wanted to find out what it was to see if she could help. However, just as she was about to excuse herself and go to the counter, Camilla emerged from the kitchen.

Camilla smiled briefly at Tom and he nodded, then they walked over and joined Honey and Dane at the table.

'Are we crashing your romantic meal?' Tom asked, looking a bit sheepish.

'No, not at all. We said you should join us.'

'How are the kittens?' Dawn asked as she joined them too.

'Snuggled up in one of the crates in the surgery. They took a feed, along with some kitten formula, then I settled them in one of the warmest crates along with a big fluffy blanket. They'll be fine now but it's a good job you found them.'

'I can't bear to think of them being out there all alone all night.'

'Well perhaps it wasn't all night. It might only have been a few hours,' Tom suggested.

'I hope it wasn't long but even so, what if they came out and saw their mum?' Dawn grimaced.

'They'll be fine.' Tom nodded. 'Absolutely fine.'

'I'm going to encourage Rick to adopt them. I don't know if it's my hormones with Alison being so young but I feel the need to look out for the kittens too.'

'You'll be a fabulous cat mum.' Tom smiled. 'Camilla? Are you all right, angel?'

All heads turned to Camilla who was chewing at a nail and staring out the window.

'Sorry?'

'I asked if you're OK.'

'Yes. I am, thanks. Just a bit tired.'

Honey took in how pale Camilla was, how tired she seemed, and how she also looked as though she'd been crying. She hoped everything was all right between Camilla and Tom. It would be dreadful to see them split up now.

Allie came over to the table with a tray of cold drinks. 'Everything all right? I brought some more mocktails and Jordan is going to take over so I can have a break. After last night's emotional rollercoaster, I'm exhausted.'

Allie pulled a chair over from the closest table and sat down.

She looked from face to face then frowned.

'What's up? You all look troubled.'

'Do you know what?' Honey decided to try to change the subject. 'I've been thinking about adding a wedding range to Purple Hen designs. It's an area of the market I haven't tapped into yet and I'm sure there are some products I could create that would appeal to bridal parties.'

Camilla flashed her a grateful look and Honey winked.

'That's a fabulous idea.' Allie nodded. 'You could make wedding favours, wedding gifts and table decorations and… ooh, all sorts!'

'We can come up with some ideas together.' Dane smiled. 'I'd love to help you.'

'Thank you.' Honey touched his hand. 'But you'll have too much marking and planning to do, Mr Ackerman.'

Dane rolled his eyes and sighed dramatically. 'Don't remind me. But I will help as much as I can during the holidays.'

'Did I hear something about weddings?'

'Chris!' Allie stood up. 'I didn't see you come in.'

'I know, you were gazing intently at Camilla.'

'Was I?'

Chris nodded.

'Take my chair and I'll get you a drink.'

'No you won't. I'm sure you've been on your feet since you got here. Anyway, I'm not stopping, I just came for the car keys.'

'Why where are you going?'

'I have some errands to run.' Chris waved a hand dismissively. 'Just need to get some more printer paper and a few other bits.'

'OK, love. The keys are in my bag in the kitchen.'

'Great.'

Chris went through to the kitchen and Camilla's eyes widened.

'What is it?' Honey asked, reaching under the table to take her hand. 'You look like you've seen a ghost.'

'No... it's not that... I... I think I left the iron on at your house, Tom.'

Tom frowned. 'Did you even use the iron this morning?'

'I did. I'm sure I did.' Camilla covered her mouth with her hand. 'Yes... oh, now I'm not sure but I won't be able to rest until I check. I'd better go.' She stood up then glanced at the door to the kitchen. 'Now!'

'I'll come with you, Camilla.' Tom drained his glass then stood up. 'Thanks for the drinks, Allie. See you all later.' He flashed a smile but it was obvious that he was worried by Camilla's odd behaviour.

As they left the café, Chris emerged from the kitchen, and now it was his face that had turned pale.

Chapter 24
Allie

Allie shared frowns and shrugs with Dawn, Honey and Tom. It was turning out to be one of the strangest days she'd experienced in a long time and Camilla's behaviour was quite troubling.

'I've got the keys.' Chris appeared at her side. His voice sounded different, quieter and strained, as if he was speaking over the phone on a bad connection. He stood there, his one hand dangling the keys and his other hand clenching and unclenching.

'What's up?' Allie tapped his hand. 'Have you got cramp?'

'No.' He shook his head then took a deep breath. 'No, I'm great. Everything's... great.'

'Okaaaay...' Allie stood up then walked him to the door. 'Are you sure you're all right?'

'Yeah.' He rubbed his hands over his face then through his hair. 'Allie, you would tell me if you were worried about something wouldn't you?'

'What like about Mandy?'

'Yes. But... I meant if there was anything else you'd

found out and you wanted to tell me but were a bit worried about how I'd react.'

Allie blinked. What on earth was he talking about?

'Of course.'

Chris cupped her chin in his hands and gently stroked her cheeks. 'You don't need to keep anything from me, you know? I'm with you in all of this and I love you. Anything that ...arises... we can deal with it together.'

'I know.' She closed her eyes as he kissed her.

'I won't be long but if you need me, call me. I'll keep an eye on my mobile. Perhaps we can have a good chat later on?'

'Yep, no problem.'

He opened the door and Allie watched him until he was out on the road.

It really was a very strange day indeed, almost as if aliens had come to earth and taken over the bodies of her friends and loved ones.

∽

'Hello?' Allie called as she entered the cottage and closed the door behind her. 'Chris?'

There was no answer, so she swapped her shoes for her slippers in the hallway then padded through to the kitchen. Mandy was at the table drinking coffee and flicking through a magazine.

'Hiya, love, how are you feeling?'

Allie was glad to see that Mandy had dressed and even had a pair of Allie's trainers on.

'I'm OK, thanks, Mum. Tired but more with it than I was this morning.'

'I'm so happy to hear that. Are you hungry?'

'Not really but I'm going to have pizza with Jordan and Max this evening and watch a movie.'

'Oh!' Allie went to the fridge and looked inside, keen to hide her delight. 'That's nice.'

'You don't mind, do you?'

Allie closed the fridge. 'Why would I mind?'

'Well, I know you like having me home.'

'Oh, love, I do but that's not to say you can't go and spend the evening with your brother. It will do you good. Jordan and Max are fabulous company.'

Mandy nodded.

'I don't suppose I could... uh...'

'You need some cash?'

'This is so embarrassing but I don't have any money left in my purse and there's no cashpoint in the village.'

'It's no problem.' Allie went through to the hall and located her bag then pulled some notes from her purse. Back in the kitchen, she handed them to her daughter. 'Just have fun.'

'I feel like a teenager again.' Mandy chewed her bottom lip.

'Come here my little girl.' Allie hugged Mandy tight, stroking her soft blonde hair and breathing in her sweet floral scent. She'd do anything for her children and even though they were both in their twenties, they'd always be her babies. 'Now go have some fun.'

'Jordan said that if it's late, I can stay over to save walking back.'

'Just text me so I know what you're doing.'

Mandy nodded. 'Will do.'

Mandy left the kitchen and Allie leant against the unit, listening to the familiar sounds of the cottage, from the clock in the hallway to the floorboards upstairs as they settled, and the swishing of the trees outside the kitchen window as the evening breeze picked up. Her whole body ached and the idea of sinking into a hot bath was very appealing. But first she wanted to know where Chris was.

She checked her mobile but he hadn't sent any texts or tried to ring so she went to her favourites and pressed call.

'Hello?'

'Chris? Where are you?'

'Just pulled up outside. Be right in.'

Allie ended the call and placed her mobile on the worktop. She heard the front door open and Chris walked in carrying several bags of shopping and a box of printer paper.

'You went food shopping?'

'Yeah… thought we needed a few bits and bobs.'

'Lovely.'

He put the bags on the worktop then shrugged out of his jacket.

'Is that why you were gone for so long?'

Allie did trust Chris but old fears and doubts from her past made her wary, even when she thought she'd managed to push them aside. Chris did everything he could to make her feel loved, but her first husband, Roger, had done a lot of damage, and she wondered sometimes if she'd ever fully escape his shadow, and what it would take to feel fully confident about her relationship.

Chris came to her and slid his strong arms around her waist. She rested her head against his chest and listened to his strong regular heartbeat. She loved him so much and losing him would break her.

'Allie?'

She looked up and met his brown eyes. They searched her face and he opened his mouth as if to speak, then he sighed instead.

'Why don't you go and have a nice bath and I'll make us some dinner?'

'That's an offer I can't refuse.'

'Good.' He smiled but there was something in his eyes that made her heart flutter; he was worried about something. 'Just... don't have the water too hot.'

As she accepted a long kiss then slipped from his embrace, she couldn't help but wonder what was on his mind. And since when had he ever worried about the temperature of her bath water?

∼

The delicious aromas of steak, mushrooms and garlic, sizzling in the frying pan met Allie as she entered the kitchen. The table in the corner was laid with pretty vintage style flower-patterned napkins, stainless steel cutlery and crystal wine glasses. A thick ivory candle burned in the centre, its light casting a warm glow on the ceiling above the table.

'Wow! What did I do to deserve this?' Allie went to Chris and hugged him from behind. He squeezed her hands then turned in her embrace.

'You're a very special lady and I love you. Do I need another reason to make you dinner?'

'Well... no. But this is just lovely.'

It wasn't the first time Chris had made her dinner but usually she knew about it in advance, as they discussed their dinner plans and did the weekly food shop together.

'I think the steaks are ready, Allie.'

Chris kissed her head then turned back to the frying pan. Allie went to the table and sat down, noting the olive-wood salad bowl full of dark green spinach, juicy red vine tomatoes, fat green olives and thick slices of cucumber.

Chris set the steaks and mushrooms on two plates and brought them to the table then he went to the fridge and brought out a bottle. When he placed it in front of her, Allie read the label, expecting a pinot grigio or a sauvignon. She wasn't sure why he'd gone for white, as they had plenty of reds in the wine wrack that would go well with steak, but the label told her it was non-alcoholic wine.

'Are we cutting down?' She pointed at the bottle.

Chris nodded. 'Think it's best.'

'Right.'

What is going on?

Chris poured the sparkling drink into the glasses then handed one to her.

'To us.'

'To us.'

They clinked glasses then drank.

'I feel a bit underdressed now to be honest.' Allie looked down at her fluffy pink pyjamas and her beige slipper boots.

'You look beautiful, as always, and I would prefer you to be comfy. Besides, I love you in those soft pjs.' He winked at her and the familiar warm glow of love and desire for him flickered in her belly.

'Before we eat...' Chris took another sip of his drink. 'I need to ask you something.'

'OK.'

Allie put her cutlery down and rested her hands in her lap.

'Allie... for a while now, I've been trying to ask you something but we always get interrupted or I feel that it's not quite the right time.'

She watched him carefully, running her gaze over the

familiar lines of his strong jaw, his straight nose, his salt and pepper hair and his deep dark eyes. It was a face she'd known since childhood and one she had missed when he'd disappeared from her life. When he'd walked back into her world last summer, everything had changed except her feelings for him; they were back and more powerful than ever. Chris had become a part of her life that she couldn't bear to lose.

'Yes… see… I'm going to ask now but I don't want you to think it's because of what I found out today. If you thought that, I'd be devastated. Because it's *not* about what I discovered today; it's about how much I love you and because I want to spend the rest of my life with you. I want you always, Allie, do you understand that?'

She nodded, her throat tightening with emotion. She was torn between wondering what he wanted to ask her and wanting to know what he'd found out today. Oh god! He wasn't ill was he? Was she going to lose him to some horrid illness or had he been asked to go abroad to work on a movie adaptation of one of his books, so she wouldn't see him for months, even years, at a time?

'Chris… you're kind of scaring me a bit here.'

He shook his head.

'No, my angel. Don't be scared. I love and adore you and you are my world. See, that's why…' He got up and pushed his chair back then pulled something from his pocket. When he dropped to his knees, then took her left hand, Allie gasped.

'Allie, will you be my wife?'

She held his gaze, her heart reaching out to him and enveloping him with love.

'Of course I will!'

Chris smiled, his eyes shining, then he slid a beautiful

platinum band with a large square diamond onto her ring finger.

'Thank you.' He kissed her hand.

'Thank you for asking.' She leant forwards and kissed him, running her hands over his face, through his hair and over his broad shoulders.

When she leant back to look at him, he was frowning.

'What is it?'

'I know this isn't very romantic but my knee has locked.' He grimaced.

'Oh no!'

Allie got up and took his hands and helped him to stand.

'You're not that old, Chris.'

'I know but it's my old footy injury plus the hours I spend sitting at a desk writing. It's not conducive to spending any length of time kneeling.'

'We'll have to get you to Honey's yoga classes. Keep you supple.'

He sat on his chair again and smiled. 'Oh, so you want me more flexible do you?'

Allie laughed.

'It's meant to be good anyway, isn't it? You know for...' He pressed his lips together.

'For what?'

'That's the other thing I wanted to speak to you about.'

Allie waited, wondering what he meant.

'Today, when I came to the café to get the car keys, I found something in your bag.'

Allie frowned. Had she left an open bar of chocolate in there again? The last time she'd done that, Chris had thought one of the cats had used her bag as a litter tray. Or had he found her bag of old pound coins that she'd been carrying round for ages? Pound coins that were no longer legal tender and that she kept forgetting about.

'I was going to propose before I found it and when I did, it didn't affect my intention, except maybe to strengthen it... because I love you and would love you whatever happened. Even if it was really unexpected. As this was.'

Why was he speaking in such a stilted way? As if he was having trouble processing his thoughts into words that wouldn't offend her.

'Allie, I found the test.'

'Test?'

He nodded.

'What test?' Allie was trying to think about what he could be referring to.

'The pregnancy test.'

Allie giggled. 'I haven't done a pregnancy test.'

Chris pulled his chair closer to the table and took her hands. 'You don't have to hide it from me, Allie. I know that you're pregnant and I'm happy about it. Honestly. We'll do this together.'

'I'm not pregnant.' She broke eye contact and stared at the steak on her plate, the mushrooms fat and gleaming, and cooling rapidly in front of her.

'But why did you have a positive test in your bag?'

She shook her head. 'I have no idea. It's the strangest thing. You're not having me on are you?'

'No. I wouldn't joke about something this serious.'

'Of course not.'

'I'll show you.'

Chris got up and went out into the hall. When he came back, he was brandishing a small white stick.

'This isn't yours?' he asked as he sat down.

Allie took the stick and stared at the twin blue lines.

'It's not mine.' She looked up at him. 'Oh no... are you disappointed? It's just you said you were happy about it and now you know I'm not and... did you want a baby then, Chris?'

He took the stick from her and shook his head.

'No, I really didn't. It's not that we're both in our forties, because that doesn't matter these days, but your children are grown up and you have the café and I have my writing and... well... there are things we want to do. If you had been expecting then I would have been happy and we would have managed, adapted our lives, but knowing that you're not is actually a relief.'

'Thank goodness for that. I wouldn't want to disappoint you.'

'You never could.'

'So where did this come from?'

'I have no idea and that's why we both really need to wash our hands. Someone peed on that stick and we don't know who it was.'

He laughed then helped her to her feet, took the stick from her and placed it on the windowsill then led her to the sink where they both gave their hands a thorough washing.

'Right then my beautiful fiancée,' Chris said as he handed her a towel, 'Shall we eat our first meal as an engaged couple before it gets really cold?'

'Yes, I can't wait.'

And they sat down together, clinked glasses once more, then ate the meal that Chris had prepared. The candlelight flickered, the bubbles in the non-alcoholic wine winked at the brims of the glasses, the diamond sparkled on Allie's left hand, and she fell even deeper in love with Chris

He would have been happy if she was expecting their baby, even though it hadn't been in their plans. He was, however, glad that she wasn't, and that was a relief for Allie. She wanted Chris all to herself and to enjoy the things they had planned, like holidaying in hot destinations, driving across America and drinking champagne in New York.

The difference was, that now she would be able to do it as Chris's wife.

Chapter 25

Dawn

Dawn hurried up the path to the café. It was early morning and she was quite tired after the events of the previous day, but Allie had sent a text late last night asking to meet her and Camilla first thing. Allie had said it was urgent, but she couldn't tell them anything else until they were face to face.

It was another beautiful morning, the air fragrant with spring flowers and the garden of the café was an array of bright colours, with forget-me-nots, tulips and crocuses in the borders and the tree to the left of the cafe was heavy with pale pink blossom that drifted gently to the grass in the light morning breeze.

Dawn pushed open the door and went inside then closed it behind her. Allie was sitting on the leather sofa to the right of the entrance and Camilla was next to her. The familiar smells of coffee and baking met her nostrils and her mouth watered.

'Morning.' Dawn took one of the chairs opposite the sofa. 'What's this about then?'

She met Allie's eyes.

'Would you like a drink first?'

Dawn shook her head. 'Better not. Alison is due a feed soon, so I can't stay long. Thought I'd get here asap then head back before she wakes.' She crossed her fingers. 'Hopefully! Or Rick'll have an early-morning earful and boy can she make a racket when she wants something. Wilful little thing she is. Just like her auntie.'

'Ha ha!' Camilla poked out her tongue.

'This won't take long.' Allie picked up her bag from the floor next to the sofa and opened it. 'I just wanted to find out if either of you know anything about this.'

She pulled out a small clear plastic bag with something inside it.

'What is it?' Dawn peered at the bag.

'Take a closer look.'

Allie handed her the bag and Dawn blew out her cheeks. 'Ah...' She passed the bag to Camilla and her sister's face crumpled.

'It's mine.' Camilla sniffed. 'Sorry, Allie. I did the test here yesterday then dropped it into your bag when Tom came in because I couldn't face telling him.'

'You're pregnant?' Allie asked and Camilla and Dawn nodded, as Allie wrapped an arm around Camilla. 'Well that's a good thing, surely?'

'Is it? It certainly wasn't planned.'

'Well sometimes that's how it happens.'

'Look at Alison.' Dawn nodded. 'And what a lovely surprise she was.'

'I'm not sure Tom is ready for this though.'

'He loves you.' Allie rubbed Camilla's arm. 'He'll be happy.'

'You think?' Camilla raised red eyes to meet Allie's, so she nodded.

'He will. He's a good man and he loves you.'

Camilla accepted a tissue from Dawn and wiped her eyes then blew her nose.

'Sorry you found that in your bag. I meant to let you know but I was so distracted last night. When we got back, Tom had brought the kittens into the house to keep an eye on them and I was busy trying to act as though I wasn't worried about anything, then I fell asleep on the sofa... I'm just so tired at the moment... and before I knew it, Tom was waking me to go up to bed and that was that.'

'I didn't find it.' Allie grimaced.

'Who did?' Camilla asked.

'Chris.'

'Oh no!' Dawn gasped.

'He thought it was mine.'

'What did you tell him?' Camilla sat up straight. 'Does he know it's mine?'

'Well, no, because I wasn't sure whose it was. I had an idea but thought I'd find out first.'

'Thank goodness for that.'

'It made for an interesting evening.' Allie laughed. 'When are you going to tell Tom?'

Camilla stared at her jeans and splayed her fingers over her legs as if they had the answer to her worries.

'Camilla?' Dawn prompted.

'Today. I have to, don't I? Things like this have a way of getting out and I don't want him finding out from anyone else.'

'Good.'

They sat in silence for a few minutes, mulling over what had happened and what was to come. The café had seen so many important moments in their lives, including revelations and confessions, laughter and tears, hopes and dreams.

It had even seen the recent arrival of little Alison and that had been an eventful day indeed!

'Allie?'

'Yes, Dawn.'

'Do you have something to tell us?'

'Uh... like what?' Allie smiled at Dawn.

'Well I'm surprised you can even lift your left hand today.'

'What? Why?'

'Wow!' Camilla grabbed Allie's hand and held it up then turned it from side to side. 'Look at the size of that diamond.'

'Are you...'

'Engaged?' Allie nodded. 'Yes!'

'EEEK! Congratulations!' Dawn and Camilla enveloped Allie in a group hug then the three of them laughed and cried as Allie filled them in on the details.

'What wonderful news,' Dawn said when she sat back in her seat. 'I'm going to be an auntie and my best friend is getting married. It's going to be an exciting year.'

'Indeed it is.' Allie nodded.

'Oh shit,' Camilla buried her head in her hands. 'I can't believe I'm going to be a mum.'

Chapter 26
Camilla

Back at Tom's cottage, Camilla sat on the floor in front of the sofa with HP's head in her lap. He was snoring gently, his pink tongue sticking out the side of his mouth and Camilla was absently stroking his velvety ears. The kittens were snuggled up in a cardboard box on her other side, enjoying the luxury of full bellies and their fleecy blanket.

When Camilla had returned from the café, Tom had told her he had an emergency appointment coming in and he'd rushed off to the surgery, but he'd promised to be back as soon as he could. Camilla had been glad of the time alone to get her thoughts in order. Allie and Dawn had helped her to prepare for telling Tom and she knew she had to get it done, but every time she thought about saying the words, her stomach rolled. She was so afraid of ruining what they had, of taking the shine off their lovely relationship by bringing another dimension to it. Even if it was their own child.

What if the news came between them and Tom drifted away from her? It had taken her so long to trust him with her heart and to let her guard down that the idea of going back to how she used to be was abhorrent. Camilla didn't want to be that woman anymore, to be afraid and hesitant; she wanted to be the woman she had started to become: happy, confident and trusting.

She heard the front door creak open and she pulled air deep into her lungs.

This was it then.

It was make or break time; the moment when she'd find out if Tom wanted her and their baby.

Tom appeared in the doorway, his cheeks flushed and his eyes bright. He always looked like this after he'd helped an animal; it was happiness and pride and Camilla knew that he loved his job. His joy in it was one of the things she loved about him. He was straightforward, uncomplicated, decent and honest. And absolutely gorgeous, of course.

'Everything all right?' he asked as he came over and kissed her, being careful not to disturb HP.

'Yes they've all been out cold since you left.'

He sat next to HP and the dog's nose twitched then he opened his eyes a fraction, showing he was aware that his master had returned home.

'It's OK, HP, don't get up to greet me or anything.'

HP's little tail wiggled but he stayed where he was.

'He loves you as much as I do.' Tom rubbed HP's back. 'You're his mum now.'

'His mum?' Camilla coughed, the word almost choking her.

What a word to choose...

'Yes, of course. You're part of his pack.'

'Right.'

'That's OK isn't it? You're happy to be here with us?'

'I am, Tom. I love you both dearly.' She reached out and took his hand. 'Was everything OK at the surgery?'

'Yes, and it wasn't exactly life or death, more a case of blocked anus glands.'

'Whose?'

'Mrs Gilchrist's poodle.'

'Ah. So you squeezed them?'

'Yep. Apparently she thought the way Penelope was dragging her behind around on the best rug was down to something far more serious.'

'I expect it was for the rug.'

'Ha! Ha! Yes.'

'Tom?'

'Hey, what's up, Camilla? Why the frown?' He stroked her cheek. 'And don't worry these hands have been thoroughly scrubbed.'

'I need to tell you something.'

'You can tell me anything.'

'I hope so because this is kind of a big something and I'm terrified it's going to come between us.'

Tom squeezed her hand. 'Nothing could ruin what we have unless you tell me you've cheated on me or are in love with someone else. And then it would be pistols at dawn. For me and him, not you, obviously.'

Camilla ran her eyes over his handsome face, taking a mental snapshot of his happy relaxed expression and burning it into her mind, just in case she never saw it again. In case what she was about to tell him changed the way he looked at life and the way he looked at her.

'Tom... I'm... I'm... I'm pregnant.'

She closed her eyes and held her breath, but the world didn't crash down around her ears and Tom didn't jump up and run for the door leaving burn marks on the wooden floorboards. Instead, when she opened her eyes, he was still there holding her hand and smiling at her, but now his eyes were glistening.

'I'm so sorry.' She scanned his face, trying to read him.

He blinked but didn't reply.

'Tom? I said I'm sorry. It was an accident and I'm not fully sure how it happened but I've done a test and it was positive and I suppose I really should do another one just to be sure, but I was a afraid to and I only found out yesterday and I've been trying to think of a way to tell you and... and...'

Tom gently moved HP off her lap then pulled her to him. He wrapped his arms around her and held her tight. She breathed in his scent, felt his love and his strength enveloping her and knew that it was OK. Everything was going to be just fine.

'Best news ever.' Tom said as he ran soft kisses down her neck. 'We're going to be parents.'

'We are. Are you sure you're OK with that?'

He got up and helped her up too.

'You've made me a very happy man, Camilla. Now let's leave HP to kitten sit while we take some time out upstairs.'

'Will the kittens be OK?'

'Did you see him with them this morning? I swear HP thinks he's their dad.'

So Camilla allowed Tom to lead her up to his bedroom, where he showed her exactly how tenderly he could love her and how much he treasured her — with his whole heart.

~

The next morning, Camilla woke to find the bedroom at Tom's cottage turned the colour of warm honey with early morning sunlight. He had opened the curtains and the window that overlooked his pretty back garden, and the air that whispered into the bedroom was filled with birdsong and the scent of spring flowers from the hanging baskets and pots on his decking. She stretched out and turned over to greet him but he wasn't there.

She sat up and listened.

From downstairs came the sound of Tom singing a song she thought she recognised. But he was doing it badly. She giggled. He was many things, but a great singer was not one of them.

Swinging her legs over the edge of the bed, she grabbed Tom's big T-shirt from the floor and pulled it on. She went to the bathroom, swilled her face then padded across the landing to the top of the stairs.

'I thought I heard you up and about. Get back to bed!' Tom said from the bottom of the staircase.

'What? Why?'

'Go on and you'll see.' He smiled up at her, looking early-morning cute in his stripy pyjama bottoms and pale blue T-shirt with his dark hair sticking up.

'OK then.'

She went back to the bedroom, climbed into bed and pulled the covers up. The bed was still warm, smelling of lavender fabric softener and of them. It was comforting, this shared space where they made love and slept and she wished she never had to leave.

Thinking back to last night, her stomach fluttered. Confessing to Tom about the accidental pregnancy had been tough but he'd been so accepting, so calm and wonderfully happy about it, as if it was all fine and would be even better. Camilla wanted to believe that it would be; she loved Tom and wanted to think that they could be a family but she was still scared that bringing a baby into the equation would disturb the lovely balance they'd created.

Time would tell.

She heard Tom padding up the stairs, then the sound of panting as HP plodded across the landing and up to the bed. He had a good sniff around then came to her, licking her outstretched hand and grinning up at her. His big brown eyes were so warm and kind and she realized that she really did love the soft old bulldog too.

'Morning HP.'

'He said he wanted to come say hello.'

'Are the kittens OK?'

Tom nodded. 'Fed and gone back to sleep. After a thorough washing from HP, that was. He's a really good mum.'

They both laughed at that and HP's little tail wagged.

'Is he coming up?'

'Bunkup, HP?' Tom asked and the dog placed his two front paws on the bed then Tom pushed him up. Once in bed, he sniffed around again before sitting next to Camilla.

'Looks like I'm redundant then.' Tom raised his eyebrows.

Camilla wrapped an arm around HP. 'You just go and get us some breakfast.'

'Actually, that's exactly what I was doing.'

'Ooh, don't let me stop you. I'm eating for two now after all.' They both froze. 'I still can't believe it, Tom.'

'Me either but you know what?'

She shook her head.

'I am over-the-moon, Camilla!'

He kissed her then headed back downstairs.

Ten minutes later, she was snuggled up to HP, thinking about the small life just beginning inside her when Tom returned, carrying a tray that he placed on the bedside table.

'For madam, we have freshly made pancakes with fresh fruit salad and maple syrup. I wasn't sure if you could face bacon.'

'That looks delicious.'

HP sat up and peered over her shoulder.

'HP thinks so too.'

'Don't let him eat your share,' Tom said. 'I'll be back in a moment with the drinks.'

Camilla lifted a plate and started to eat, enjoying the light fluffy pancakes with the sweet fresh strawberries, grapes, raspberries and blueberries. Along with the maple syrup, they were a heavenly combination. She shared a few plain pieces of pancake with HP and had almost finished when Tom returned.

'Good?'

'Amazing. Thank you! I didn't know I was so hungry.'

'No nausea this morning?' he asked as he placed a large mug of tea on the bedside table along with a glass of orange juice.

'Not so far. It's strange really. I don't feel right but I haven't felt queasy yet. As long as I relax and think pleasant thoughts, it seems to stave it off.'

'That's good.' He sighed as he walked around the bed and placed his own drinks on his bedside table.

'What?'

'It might get worse though... before it gets better.'

'I know. I've seen Dawn go through it three times.'

'Budge up HP.' Tom sat on the bed and encouraged HP to move over so he was squashed in between them. He started to pant almost immediately.

'He's too hot.' Camilla rubbed HP's velvety ears.

'I knew he would be. Come on HP.' Tom stood up and helped HP off the bed then the dog wandered into the hallway and dramatically collapsed onto the wooden boards.

'It still makes me jump when he does that.' Camilla watched HP as he stretched his short muscular legs out then settled for a snooze.

'He's a bit dramatic isn't he? Likes us to know he's there.' Tom got back into bed.

'Thank you for this delicious breakfast in bed. I should get pregnant more often.' She flashed him a smile.

'It's good news, Camilla. Really good news.'

'Did I tell you Allie's news?'

'I don't think you did.'

'My head was full of how to tell you about the baby yesterday, so it slipped my mind. She's only gone and got engaged.'

Tom's mouth slowly opened then he covered his face with his hands.

'What? What's wrong?' Camilla placed her empty glass on the table then shuffled around to face Tom.

'That's great news but lousy timing.'

'Why?'

'Because... oh Camilla, there's something I've been trying to do for ages and every time I try, something interrupts us or I have to wait. I was going to do it yesterday, then you seemed unwell and so tired, so I planned on doing it this morning... but now you've told me that and...' He blew air out of his mouth and shook his head. 'Blast it.'

'Tom,' Camilla put her hand on his arm. 'Whatever it is, you can do it. I love you. We're... going to be parents. Together.'

'And that's the other issue. I don't want you to think I'm doing it because of that either. I want to do it because I wanted to anyway, and was going to and then... you know what? I'm going to do it anyway.' He stood up and opened the drawer of his bedside table then pulled something out. He walked around the bed and stood next to Camilla.

She gazed up at him, her heart pounding with realization.

Tom lowered to his knees then took her hand.

She waited.

HP started to snore in the hallway. The birds sang in the trees outside. A plane passed overhead, the whine of its engine cutting through the peace of the morning.

'Tom? What is it?'

He shook his head but kept his eyes fixed on the wooden floor.

'Tom?'

Camilla reached out and gently raised his chin then sighed. His eyes were shining and he was biting his lower lip.

'Tom, come here.' She opened her arms and he moved into them then she hugged him tight. 'What is it? Too soon? Too much? Change of heart?' Her stomach lurched at the last question but she had to give him an out if he needed it.

'No. Course not.' His voice sounded strangled, as if the effort of speaking hurt.

'Then what?'

'Just... a lot... of emotion.' He leant back and met her eyes. 'I was, as you know, married before. But it didn't feel like this.'

'Well that's good.'

'And now... now there's a baby too.' He placed his hand on her stomach, and his palm was warm, his proximity comforting, his scent intoxicating as always.

'Yes there is. We can do this, can't we?'

He nodded.

'OK then.' Camilla raised his hand and kissed it, then slid off the bed and knelt in front of him. Holding hands, they gazed into each other's eyes, learning more about each other by the second, knowing that they were in this for the long haul, that they both wanted this more than anything.

Camilla took a deep breath.

'Tom Stone, I love and adore you. I have done since we first met, but it took me a while to accept that. I now know it with every fibre of my being. Therefore, I would be delighted if you would do me the honour of becoming my husband.'

His eyes widened. 'I was going to ask you.'

'But I got there first.' She smiled. 'That's OK, right?'

'Of course it is.'

'So...' She squeezed his hands.

'So?'

'Is there a ring?'

'Yes!' He looked around him then pulled a small black box from underneath his leg. He opened it and there, on a white satin pillow, sat a platinum ring. At the centre was a round emerald with a sparkling diamond either side of it.

'It's beautiful.'

'The emerald is to match your beautiful eyes and to remind you that I love gazing into them.'

Tom took the ring from the box then slid it onto Camilla's finger.

'How did you know the size?'

'I measured it when you were sleeping.'

'Really?'

'No!' He laughed. 'I had a look at your other rings in your jewellery box then gaged it from them.'

'It's perfect.'

'Just like you.'

They got back into bed and Tom slid his arm around her shoulders as they sipped their tea.

'I guess we have to celebrate with tea now?' Camilla held up her mug and Tom gently tapped his against it.

'I guess so.'

'That's fine by me.'

'Me too.'

'Love you.'

'Love you more.'

And they sat that way for some time, as the sun climbed in the sky, HP snored and the kittens slept soundly in their box downstairs. It was such a perfect moment that neither of them wanted to leave it until they had to.

So they didn't.

EPILOGUE - ONE SATURDAY IN JULY

The atmosphere in Jenny Talbot's small salon was electric. It was hot because of the surprise springtime heat wave that had swept across the country, and the four fans that Jenny had placed around the salon just seemed to be moving the warm air around. Jenny had also propped the front door open but the warm July morning meant that little air was coming in to help cool the place down.

There were women everywhere and Honey's head was buzzing. Even though she was a bridesmaid, Jenny had roped her in to help and she'd done everything from making coffee to plucking eyebrows to holding clips as Jenny pinned them into hair.

However, Honey had to admit that it was an exciting morning. One of her best friends in the entire world was getting married and every time she looked at the bride, her heart squeezed.

'Honey?' She resisted the urge to sigh as Jenny called her name yet again.

'Yes, Jenny.'

EPILOGUE - ONE SATURDAY IN JULY

'I think we're just about ready to open the champagne now, don't you?'

'What, you mean we're all done?'

'Yes, sweetie!' Jenny waved a hand in front of her face. 'It's so warm in here. Think we should have the bubbly on the terrace. Come on everyone, outside!'

As Jenny ushered her friends and clients outside, their heels click clacking in unison as they went, Honey got the two bottles of champagne from the fridge in the small kitchen. She stood in front of the open fridge and let the cold air drift out over her legs and toes. Her toes looked really pretty with their pearly-pink nail polish that complimented her strappy white high-heeled sandals. Honey wasn't much of a one for wearing heels, but these were so pretty that they made it worth the discomfort. The sandals had been chosen to match her pale pink bridesmaid's dress. It was made of silk and chiffon, in a Jane Austen style with short sleeves, a fitted bust and a skirt that fell from below the bust to the floor. It had two knee-high side slits so her sandals could be seen when she moved or sat down. She had a necklace of tiny freshwater pearls and matching dropper earrings, revealed today by her hairstyle, with some of her bobbed hair clipped back from her face and the rest falling in soft sausage curls. Jenny had put in more purple and pink streaks before styling her hair, so it now complimented the dress perfectly.

She'd left Dane at their cottage two hours earlier and wouldn't see him again until they met at the café for the ceremony, so he hadn't seen her dress or her hair yet and she couldn't wait to find out what he thought. She was getting used to enjoying his compliments and the way he looked at her, as if she was the most beautiful woman he'd ever seen, and she knew she'd always appreciate it. This was the first

EPILOGUE - ONE SATURDAY IN JULY

wedding they'd attended together and it was going to be a very special day.

She carried the bottles outside and placed them on the table that Jenny had set up outside the village salon. Dawn had already brought the glasses out, so Honey popped one of the corks then started to pour, assisted by Allie's mum, Connie, who was positively radiant in a light blue dress and matching jacket.

~

Dawn looked around at her friends and family. Seeing her daughter, Laura, in her bridesmaid's dress and her mum, Jackie, sporting a cream and gold outfit with a matching hat that would've made the Queen proud, was making her emotional enough, but seeing Honey, Allie and Camilla all dressed up too was enough to tip her over the edge of the emotional precipice. If she tumbled over, she didn't think she'd ever come back. Seeing as how she didn't want to ruin her makeup, she picked up a flute of champagne and took a swig. Even though she was still breastfeeding, Dawn thought a sip of bubbly would be OK on this special occasion, then she'd stick to soft drinks for the rest of the day.

The champagne was cool and crisp and it fizzed in her belly, increasing her feeling of euphoria. She'd left Rick and James at home that morning, taking Laura and Alison with her to the salon. Her daughters were both wearing pretty gowns that matched those of the older bridesmaids, but with fuller skirts. It had been hard work getting Laura and James away from the cats they had adopted back in the spring, as her children adored Meowly Cyrus and William Shakespaw. Camilla and Tom had helped them to choose names for the then kittens, and Dawn found them highly amusing whenever she had to call the cats in for their dinner.

Alison was currently napping in her pram just inside the door of the salon, which was a good thing as Dawn knew she'd be ready for the ceremony at noon. Rick and James would meet them at the café because James was a pageboy and Rick was best man. He'd been delighted to be asked and was taking his role seriously. He had looked so handsome in his light grey suit with the silver tie and Dawn had given him a long tender kiss before leaving home.

Honey finished filling glasses then raised her own.

'Ladies!' She cleared her throat. 'I would like to make a toast to the bride. When I came to Heatherlea, my life was very different. I was lonely, directionless and had never really known what true friendship was. Then one day, I went to the café and met three wonderful women. Now my life is so full of love and happiness that I count my blessings every day. Thank you my dear friends for your love and support. Thank you Jenny for making us all look rather fancy. Here's to the beautiful bride and to her lifetime of happiness! You deserve it, sweetheart!'

They raised their glasses: 'To the bride and to a lifetime of happiness.'

They took it in turns to say a few words, and Dawn smiled at the warmth of this circle of women. Laura came and stood next to her then gave her a hug, and Dawn's throat tightened even more.

This was a beautiful start to what would hopefully be a beautiful day, a day when she'd see two people she adored agreeing to spend the rest of their lives together.

EPILOGUE - ONE SATURDAY IN JULY

Camilla held her skirts up with one hand and her bouquet in the other. The dress was so beautiful and she didn't want to get the hem dusty or to snag it on any stones. She was a combination of excited and nervous, a strange feeling but it was such a special day. She hadn't been sure that the silk and chiffon dress would suit her but when she'd gone for the final fitting, and saw how it fell from her bust to her feet, she'd known that it was a perfect dress for her baby bump. She was nearly five months along now and everything was going well. The horrid morning sickness had disappeared at around fourteen weeks and she'd had two scans to confirm that everything was OK with the baby. She and Tom had agreed that they didn't want to find out the gender of the baby but at the second scan it had been impossible to ignore the fact that they were having a son. Tom had grinned at her when they'd seen the evidence on the monitor then he'd kissed her and told her how happy he was. His happiness matched her own. The pregnancy might have been a shock but Camilla wouldn't change a thing now. She was getting more and more excited about the prospect of motherhood every day and had started to prepare one of the bedrooms as a nursery after she'd rented out her cottage and moved in with Tom.

When they neared the street of The Cosy Cottage Café, the women slowed down and Jenny did a quick check of dresses, hair and makeup.

'Time for us to go and join everyone else,' Jackie said, as she hugged her daughters and granddaughter, while Connie hugged Allie.

The older women headed to the café, then the remaining women got into the order in which they were going to enter the café garden to walk along the aisle that Jordan and Max had created.

EPILOGUE - ONE SATURDAY IN JULY

'You all look so perfect,' Jenny said. She took some photographs on her mobile phone, including a selfie with her in, then she hugged them all quickly. It had been agreed that guests would take lots of photo on their mobiles or with their own cameras then send them to the bride and groom, and the money that would have been spent on a photographer would go to a local charity instead. 'Right, ladies, are we ready?

'Yes,' they said in unison.

'I'll go and let them know you're ready.'

Jenny gave a wave then hurried off along the road, going as fast as her gold platform heels and tight red satin dress would allow her to move.

This was it then... the wedding was about to begin...

∽

Allie breathed deeply, trying to fill her lungs with the warm fragranced July air. She couldn't believe the day had arrived. This wedding had taken quite a lot of planning and preparation, in spite of it being a relatively small affair, with friends and close family as guests and the rest of the village invited to join in the celebrations at the café afterwards.

'Do I look all right?' she asked.

'Mum, you look amazing. Everyone does.' Mandy smiled. She was looking so much better herself, Allie thought, as she took in her daughter's glossy hair and rosy cheeks. Her heartbreak had knocked her down but just as Allie had hoped, Mandy had got back up and was almost back to her best. Almost. She'd returned to London and her job after a week but had come home every other weekend since Easter, something that had delighted Allie, Chris and Jordan. They hadn't seen so much of Mandy in years, but it

EPILOGUE - ONE SATURDAY IN JULY

was as if running to her family when she was at her lowest ebb, had reminded her how much she loved and needed them, and it had definitely brought them all much closer. Allie wouldn't have seen Mandy hurt for all the world but she couldn't deny that seeing more of her daughter again was absolutely wonderful.

She took Mandy's hand and they walked along the pavement to the café then slowed before they reached the gate. Allie opened her arms and hugged her daughter then hugged Dawn, Camilla and Honey. Their shared friendship and the love and support they offered one another had carried them all through some tough times and that made the good times all the more special.

And now, there was to be a wedding at The Cosy Cottage Café.

~

Allie watched as her friends took their places in front of her, starting with Dawn and her two daughters, with baby Alison in her pram, the hood of which had been decorated with white roses, sweetpeas and ribbons. Next was Camilla, then Honey. The three of them were like beautiful angels in their pale pink gowns with their happy smiles and sparkling eyes.

Mandy took her arm and as if by magic, Jordan appeared at her other side. Her children had agreed to walk her along the aisle. Her father could have done it, but as Mandy and Jordan were older now, they'd decided that this would be their way of showing that they trusted Chris to love and care for their mum.

'Ready?' Jordan asked.

She met his eyes and nodded. 'I'm ready.'

EPILOGUE - ONE SATURDAY IN JULY

'Ladies.' He gestured at the café.

The gate to the café was open ready, and the murmur of conversation in the garden faded as the enchanting melody of a harp floated through the air, playing an instrumental version of Christina Perri's *A Thousand Years*.

The bridesmaids made their way along the aisle first, and from either side of the path, the guests smiled and nodded their approval. Jordan and Mandy led Allie to the gate and she looked up to find all eyes on her. She smiled at her mum and dad and at her friends, then her gaze was drawn to the door of the café, where under an arch of cream roses and purple lavender, Chris was waiting.

And from that moment, she saw nothing except for Chris.

As she walked towards him, with Jordan whispering under his breath: 'Right together, left together,' the years fell away and memories of time spent with Chris flashed before her eyes. Laughing as he handed her an ice cream from the van, then when he turned with his own, the top scoop of vanilla falling from his cone and landing on his black T-shirt. Giggling hard after they'd been caught in a summer thunderstorm in the park, their clothes soaked through. Baking together in the café kitchen, then Chris sliding his arms around her waist and kissing her neck, flour everywhere as she turned in his arms and held him tight.

When she reached his side, Mandy and Jordan kissed her and Mandy took her simple lavender bouquet, then they went and sat next to their grandparents.

Chris took her hand and kissed it.

'You're so beautiful, Allie.'

She was glad that she'd chosen the simple silver gown made of silk and chiffon. It was light and floaty and cut in the same style as the bridesmaids' dresses. Her blonde hair

EPILOGUE - ONE SATURDAY IN JULY

had been gently curled and she wore a silver headband set with grey and cream freshwater pearls.

'You look pretty good too, Chris.'

And he did, in his white shirt, lavender waistcoat, light-grey jacket and matching trousers. His salt and pepper hair was cropped short and his brown eyes were warm and familiar as they roamed over Allie, making her tummy flip with love and happiness.

The majority of the ceremony took place in the café garden under the flowered arch, but Allie, Chris and their chosen witnesses, Camilla and Tom, had to go inside the café, along with the registrar and her assistant, for the contracting and declaratory words.

When they emerged from the café as husband and wife, they were met with cheers and applause, and handfuls of rose petal confetti. Chris led Allie across the lawn to the area they'd had set up as a dancefloor and there, before their family and friends, he lifted her and twirled her round then lowered her, cupped her face in his smooth hands and kissed her.

It had taken them half a lifetime to get to this moment and to be married, but now they were joined together for the rest of their lives and Allie wouldn't have it any other way.

~

The dancing went on all afternoon, and guests enjoyed a summery buffet made up of local produce. Allie and Chris had worked hard through the week to prepare the food for the buffet. Savoury dishes included lemon, asparagus and ricotta tart, herby salmon and couscous parcels and the local butcher had brought a large mustard-roasted beef fillet as a

EPILOGUE - ONE SATURDAY IN JULY

wedding present. For dessert there were mini lemon meringue pies, red cherry bakewell tarts and white chocolate berry cheesecakes. Mandy had insisted on having the wedding cake made by a friend of hers in London. It was a beautiful three-tiered chocolate cake with rich shiny chocolate frosting and juicy red strawberries dotted around the sides.

Jordan and Max served the drinks, including pink champagne, rum punch with slices of lemon, lime and orange, and there was freshly-made cloudy lemonade or virgin mojitos for the children and those adults not drinking alcohol.

As the sky darkened and stars appeared like diamond pinpricks set in ebony silk, Chris and Allie wandered away from the dance floor and over to the pergola, which was fragrant with honeysuckle and roses. Tea lights flickered in colourful jars on the tables under the pergola and the fairy lights draped around the pergola and the trees twinkled. The air was intoxicating and Allie couldn't tell if it was the champagne she'd drunk, the heady scent from the flowers or the fact that she was so happy making her feel lightheaded.

Chris slid his arms around her waist and gazed into her eyes.

'Thank you for making me the happiest man alive, Allie.'

'You've made me happier than I could ever have imagined, Chris.'

'You're my wife,' he whispered, his eyes shining as they reflected the candlelight.

'You're my husband.'

'It's how it should always have been. I love you, Allie.'

'I love you too.'

Chris lowered his head and kissed her softly, and the

EPILOGUE - ONE SATURDAY IN JULY

world around them dimmed, until it was just them and their love for each other. When they finally broke apart, Chris took her hand. 'Shall we dance?'

'I'd like that.'

And they headed back to their family and friends, to the warmth and love that the community of Heatherlea offered.

It truly had been a wonderful wedding at The Cosy Cottage Café.

The End

WANT MORE?

Visit my website here - https://rachelgriffith sauthor.com to subscribe to my newsletter, to download free short stories and find out what's next.

Take a look at ***Also by Rachel Griffiths*** for plenty more delightfully uplifting stories!

Dear Reader,

Thank you so much for reading **A Wedding at The Cosy Cottage Café**. I hope you enjoyed reading it as much as I enjoyed writing it.

Did the story make you smile, laugh or even cry? Did you care about the characters?

If you can spare five minutes of your time, I would be so grateful if you could leave a short review. Genuine word of mouth helps other readers decide whether to take a trip to **The Cosy Cottage Café** too.

Stay safe and well!

With love,

Rachel X

Acknowledgments

Firstly, thanks to my gorgeous family. I love you so much! XXX
To my friends, for your support, advice and encouragement and to everyone who has interacted with me on social media, huge heartfelt thanks.
Special thanks to Daniela Colleo of StunningBookCovers .com for the beautiful cover.
To everyone who buys, reads and reviews this book, thank you.

About the Author

Rachel Griffiths is an author, wife, mother, Earl Grey tea drinker, gin enthusiast, dog walker and fan of the afternoon nap. She loves to read, write and spend time with her family.

WANT MORE?

Visit my website here - https://rachelgriffithsauthor.com to subscribe to my newsletter, to download free short stories and find out what's next.

Take a look at ***Also by Rachel Griffiths*** for plenty more delightfully uplifting stories!

Also by Rachel Griffiths

<u>Cwtch Cove Series</u>

Christmas at Cwtch Cove

Winter Wishes at Cwtch Cove

Mistletoe Kisses at Cwtch Cove

The Cottage at Cwtch Cove

The Café at Cwtch Cove

Cake And Confetti at Cwtch Cove

A New Arrival at Cwtch Cove

A Cwtch Cove Christmas (A collection of books 1-3)

<u>The Cosy Cottage Café Series</u>

Summer at The Cosy Cottage Café

Autumn at The Cosy Cottage Café

Winter at The Cosy Cottage Café

Spring at The Cosy Cottage Café

A Wedding at The Cosy Cottage Café

A Year at The Cosy Cottage Café (The Complete Series)

<u>The Little Cornish Gift Shop Series</u>

Christmas at The Little Cornish Gift Shop

Spring at The Little Cornish Gift Shop

Summer at The Little Cornish Gift Shop

The Little Cornish Gift Shop (The Complete Series)

<u>Sunflower Street Series</u>

Spring Shoots on Sunflower Street

Summer Days on Sunflower Street

Autumn Spice on Sunflower Street

Christmas Wishes on Sunflower Street

A Wedding on Sunflower Street

A New Baby on Sunflower Street

New Beginnings on Sunflower Street

Snowflakes and Christmas Cakes on Sunflower Street

The Cosy Cottage on Sunflower Street

Snowed in on Sunflower Street

Springtime Surprises on Sunflower Street

Autumn Dreams on Sunflower Street

A Christmas to Remember on Sunflower Street

Secret Santa on Sunflower Street

Starting Over on Sunflower Street

The Dog Sitter on Sunflower Street

Autumn Skies Over Sunflower Street

A Year on Sunflower Street (Sunflower Street Books 1-4)

<u>Standalone Stories</u>

Christmas at The Little Cottage by The Sea

The Wedding

<u>The Cornish Garden Café Series</u>

Spring at the Cornish Garden Café

Summer at the Cornish Garden Café

Autumn at the Cornish Garden Café

Winter at the Cornish Garden Café

Printed in Dunstable, United Kingdom